Lock Down Publications and Ca$h
Presents

RELENTLESS
GOON 3

Love & Gunplay

Written By
PRINCE A. TAUHID

First Edition 2025

Printed in the United States of America

This is a work of fiction. Names, characters, places, and incidents either are products of the author's imagination or are used fictitiously. Any similarity to actual events or locales or persons, living or dead, is entirely coincidental.

Lock Down Publications
P.O. Box 944
Stockbridge, GA 30281
www.lockdownpublications.com

Like our page on Facebook: Lock Down Publications
www.facebook.com/lockdownpublications.ldp

Stay Connected with Us!

Text **LOCKDOWN** to 22828 to stay up-to-date with new releases, sneak peaks, contests and more…

Like our page on Facebook:
Lock Down Publications

Join Lock Down Publications/The New Era Reading Group

Visit our website:
www.lockdownpublications.com

Follow us on Instagram:
Lock Down Publications

Email Us: We want to hear from you!

Karma is a bitch, and the daughter of her's is no good either!

PROLOGUE

THE way Mitch saw the situation he was dealing with against Melvin was, he came to feel that, a proper amount of street justice was given out. This was a dish of revenge best served cold. He hit back against Melvin for everything he deemed was perpetrated on him by Melvin and his association to the main enemy of his, Mr. Raymond.

Mitch was really heated over the fact that Melvin broke one of the main rules of loyalty. This happened at the point when he reneged on his agreement and sided with the enemy. Mitch was one of those type of dudes who would hold a grudge forever.

To make matters worse, Mitch felt without a doubt, that Melvin was the evil influence behind his daughter's disrespect of him. He felt that Melvin was also behind Tisha stealing $100,000 from him and eventually buying him expensive gifts with the money. He knew Melvin had manipulated her into doing this slimy shit, because she was too weak and emotional hungover for him. Too stupid enough to do such a thing to her own daddy, Mitch reasoned. Not to mention the fact that Melvin was also the one who shot and killed Roland, Mitch's nephew. The relentless goon Melvin, took away a strong family member by default. And, while still having a hold of the daughter to use and control how he saw fit, he was winning. For this, according to Mitch, Melvin had to die!

Long before Mitch contacted Roland and put him and his boys up to the failed mission to rob and kill Melvin, he was *furious to break up the love connection between the two love birds—Melvin and Tisha.*

Mitch now seriously despised the fact that his daughter was madly in love with a dude he now madly hated. This now had him in a position to never accept the fact that this was a thing. But, there wasn't anything he could do about it. Or was it.

Mitch's plan was to have Melvin killed, but it seemed no one he hired to track him down, knew where he was, let alone have the ability to lay a hand on him. Mitch resorted to the next best option. This was to have Melvin's mother hit. She would bear the burden of her son and take his place in the lineup to be whacked.

The cold-blooded hit man had no problem knocking off an elderly woman like Mitch ordered him to do. His work was all in the name of a dollar. And he operated with no remorse and no sense of conscience. What had to be done, simply had to be done. Period!

Part One

Chapter 1

Presently...

NOW back From NYC, VICK and Melvin made their return to Miami. The trip to the north was a success. No sooner than the moment of turning on his main phone, Melvin was hit with a slew of messages Tisha had sent. It was important. They really needed to talk, she reasoned. However, she wanted to meet him at some other location, not at her place. Melvin already had a general idea on what it was about.

The conversation she was looking to have was surrounded by the fact of her dad acting like a bitch about her seeing him. He was still butt-sore behind the fact that Melvin lined up with Mr. Raymond and not him. Melvin was asked to stop by her sister Chioma's house. He gave his word he would. At 9:30 p.m. the same day, he made his way to the Carol City section of town. He now drove around in a low budget rental. He left the Tahoe parked in the garage at Vick's place, out of sight and out of mind.

Melvin's mother let him know that while he was away, some girl showed up to the house looking for him. She had her brother with her too. A guy named Calvin. The guy came again after the first visit, but alone the second time. Supposedly, they was looking for him because one of her people mentioned to them that he was home from prison and back in Miami. She claimed that she wanted to see him for herself.

Melvin wanted to wait until Vick or him again, had the drop on Calvin to whack him and have him gone forever, before he planned to bring the truck back out. Vick's hitters weren't able to track him down while they were away. He didn't want Calvin to know what type of vehicle he he drove. This had to be avoided at all costs.

Melvin texted Tisha to let her know he was at Chioma's house out front. Her Range Rover was parked there as well. She immediately sprang up off the bed out the house to meet him. She got into the car, and they rode off to take a tour of the town while they talk.

"So, what's good, sweetie? What you got on your mind you looking to talk 'bout?" he said.

"Oh, I got a whole lot I wanna talk about with you today. And I mean a lot," Tisha responded.

"Okay. Good. But don't, and I mean don't, say one word to me today, not a word, about what yo goddamn daddy done said to you about us. I don't wanna hear it, Tisha," Melvin stated. He honestly felt the need to initiate the conversation on this note.

Tisha looked at him with a sense of awe and admiration in her eyes. The thought passed through her mind of how solid they had grown together and how far they had come together. She showed a warm loving smile and then made it her business to respond to his words.

"Melvin, look, I been known for a long time that my dad would react the way he did. But I—"

"Tisha!" He cut her off to say, "I don't wanna hear it, okay."

"Okay, but all I was gonna say was, I don't seem to understand. Just because my dad has the need to take out his anger on me and you, why would he try to interfere with what we got going on? He should be happy for me behind me being happy. I would think."

"I wouldn't mind knowing why myself," Melvin replied.

The AC was blowing hard in the rental. The music was at a low and soothing volume. The track Slow Fade by the singer, Ruth B, serenaded them throughout the sound system. Tisha lip synced along with the lyrics.

She spoke again, "Melvin, the truth be, I don't really give a fuck about how my dad feels or about what he has to say 'bout me being with you. We ain't done nothing to him to be treated like this. But, I do understand why he hates Raymond though. It's not a reason to beef with you, though," she stated, then cupped Melvin underneath his chin while gently stroking him along the cheekbone.

"Well, good, that's all I needed to know, that you and me are one. Nothing or no one else matters from this point onward." Melvin respected her words."But look, on another note, what's the deal with the two of us coming together to make some money? I'm ready to get busy, sweetie." He was eager to find a way to exploit Tisha out of whatever resources she had to give. His question came off as serious minded and connected with the seriousness of how he deemed his expectations to be of what they had.

"I'm with that. I'm ready for the same thing, babe. What type of business you ready to get into?"

"Shit! Whatever that's selling the most right now, sweetie. But that cousin of yours, what does he got going on?"

"To answer you directly, we get supplied pounds of cream to sell it for the low. Also, the pills back poppin' again, along with the molly, and some other stuff," Tisha acknowledged.

"Well, if that be so, go on ahead and put things together on your end with getting the supply in place. And in the meantime, I'll be busy on my end putting people in place to get rid of the product and bringing in the money, okay?"

"All I gotta do is make some phone calls, babe, to let my people know what's what, and we're on from there." Tisha was able to convince him on exactly how easy it was for her to initiate all that they were looking to do.

"Make that happen then. Because I got people I'm in contact with up north, who's looking to connect with somebody down here to be supplied with better product at a lower price," he mentioned.

"I'll do it for you, babe. I ain't got no problem with it. And by the way, if I'm going the orders of my dad to be with you, I gotta help you get on as well, if we intent on doing this. Also, let's not forget about my hair and nail salons and other legit places and entities of business, doing damn well too." She felt the need to make Melvin aware that the illegal side of things wasn't all she had in mind to get paid for.

"I won't lose sight of that, Tisha. The idea is to continue to get money from all ends of the spectrum and grow and expand like that. Then before we know it, your businesses and the shit I got going on l, will be on the way to becoming a household name. At least here in south Florida. I got high hopes and even more ambition to be successful," he stated as best he could. He was able to relate to what she was saying.

"And I plan to be right here with you every step of the way, sweetheart. Now, let's find a spot to chill for a few hours. That way, you can fuck me real good with that big ol' dick of yours I love so much," Tisha responded.

"Other than us talkin' on business that we both have agreed on, that's something that I can agree too. Most definitely can."

The two then headed toward the South Beach area to get a hotel suite. A half hour later, they were situated inside. They ended up staying all night. Tisha was hot between the legs. They fucked like crazy. She had a winner in him, and he had a winner in her.

Chapter 2

MR. Raymond called for a high stakes meeting between his successor, the nephew Phil Jr., Emanuel, and with Willie. He wanted to discuss the new protocol that was being put in place, the one where it would be Phil Jr. that would be the one the others reported to and followed instructions from. The topic of the new format about transport would be discussed as well, since a recent seizure of a cargo boat had happened. The port was hot.

The old way they smuggled dope into the country was compromised. Señor Chucho, did not like this. He wasn't happy about losing his product. This was the material that made him a lot of money. This also was one of the first steps for American authorities towards shutting him and his operations down. Nothing was sitting well with him. He was pissed. And for the first time over the many years he's functioned, he was now on their radar.

Raymond and little Phil needed to do everything necessary to make sure that nothing happened again. Potential danger loomed if these types of mishaps continued. Mr. Raymond simply had to avoid this at all costs. Especially so, at this point with him entering the political realm and needing all the dirt of his swept under the rug.

He began, "Nephew... Emanuel... and Willie... I'm glad that y'all could make it here to talk with me on such a short notice. And as y'all know, the recent events down at the Port of Miami, made it mandatory that we do as we are now. Not only did we lose millions of dollars in supply, we also lost a few expensive caskets, ceramic pieces, and the most important part, we lost the way we transport our product to the United States from Mexico across the gulf. With this, I gotta make right before I get all the way out of the way.

"Phil Jr. now in charge. It's all him. But the old way on how we stash the material we get, is still the same. Likewise, with how we get rid of it. The only difference would now be, we gotta go to Texas to pick up shipments now, once everything crosses the border," Mr. Raymond let out. "The rest is up to your team if drivers to get it back to Miami. But it's all on you, nephew. I'm out the way. And this the reason why I brought everybody together today. So we can layout a game plan on how we gonna proceed moving forward." Mr. Raymond clearly stated what the deal was to the men he hosted.

The three guests all nodded in agreement to each word he said. He continued at that point. "The format remains the same. Emanuel got responsibility for keeping everything put up. But the floor is yours, Lil Phil. You the man now. I passed it all to you," he said, now eager to run the inherited drug empire from behind the scenes. He no longer could afford to be at the front.

"Thank you, Uncle Raymond. It's a pleasure to be here with you men. I always looked up to y'all with helping me learn my way through this area I ain't never went through before. And as we all know, unc here, done personally took me to meet the top guy down in Mexico. He's the one that gave us the opportunity to live a better life to live. Señor Chuco is a man who is dead serious about the business he runs. And I for one, must be as too. My life and the lives of my family depend on me establishing stronger business ties. And that's what I'm intent on doing. Since I know I'm the leader now, I designated somebody already to be my pickup man on the trips out to Texas. He's a dude I had on my team for a long time now. I trust him like no other. I also got two dudes that's close to me that's gonna be my personal bodyguards and do transports with my driver. So, this part I already got together. I'mma follow in the footsteps of my uncle there," Phil Jr. Stated, pointing at Mr. Raymond in gesture

He admired his elders. This was something his dad taught him before he died. The thought of his old man passed through Emanuel's mind, causing him to put on a bright smile of his own.

The meeting went on maybe an hour more, as they sipped on drinks, puffed on premium cigars, and made the bond tighter that they held. This was one of the main reasons behind the get together, in addition to Mr. Raymond passing the torch of power to the nephew in front of the other two. The foundation of the Stephens organization was strong. This was all that mattered.

Chapter 3

THE relationship that Melvin and Tisha had, got stronger by the day. This was personally and business-wise. It wasn't that he didn't love Traci no more, or didn't want to be with her. It was the fact they lived two different lives.

They really didn't have time for each other. Plus Traci was older than he was. So, this played a part in Melvin favoring the younger Tisha the way he did.

He loved Traci and wished her the best as they had no problems with each other. They simply grew apart, as he hadn't stayed over at her place as much as he had when he first got free. Nonetheless, they were still together— "per se" —and spent time with each other on her off days.

On the other hand, Melvin and Tisha spent plenty of days and nights together too. They had gone so far as to lease an apartment to share. This would be their spot to chill and be with one another, away from home and outside of anyone else trying to dig into their business. Tisha's dad Mitch, in particular. At no time had she ever really tried to hide Melvin from Mitch in that type of way. Her thing was, she wasn't gonna let her dad dictate to her who she could and couldn't be with.

Mitch had good reason to believe that the love birds were still seeing each other. Tisha made this known to Melvin about the wild random stops her dad was making by her house at crazy hours of the night. He was itching to catch Melvin there.

The father and daughter had serious arguments about his erratic behavior and about his stubborn notions. This was also the motivation as to why it was necessary for Tisha and Melvin to get the apartment they had.

Mitch's vindictive attitude and actions, prevented him from letting go of the grudge he held with Mr. Raymond and those who were associated with him. And since he had not came across Mr. Raymond since the day at the restaurant when it was announced that the club would be sold, he needed a new target. Somebody that was close to him. His anger and frustrations were now aimed at Melvin.

On this one particular Saturday night when Melvin and Tisha stayed over at the duplex apartment they leased in South Miami Heights, she let him know that her father threatened on more than one occasion, to cut her off from everything he provided her with, and wouldn't have anything more to do with her, if she continued to deal with him.

According to Mitch, this was because he felt that Melvin was more of a snake than Mr. Raymond was. He felt Melvin was only dealing with Tisha to use her, then run back to Mr. Raymond to report everything he knew on him and his family, she let Melvin know.

"Melvin, how about my dad really pissed off at the fact he knows me and you still seeing each other. But he can't quite seem to catch it. That man is so mad at the fact you decided to roll with Raymond over him, that he don't know how not let something like that make him mad," she said.

"Oh, really?" he said nonchalantly.

"Hell yeah! And, he beginning to piss me off with his bullshit! But in his words, it's not so much about you choosing to be on Raymond's team. It's the fact you chose to line up with an enemy of his. And on top of that, you still got me, his daughter."

Melvin had to laugh like at the reality of it all.

The two sat on the bed, watching an episode of The Handmaid's Tale on Hulu.

"What seems to be so funny, baby?" she asked.

Melvin didn't attempt to hide his humor over Mitch's petty reactions. He continued to laugh out loud there in Tisha's face.

"This not a laughing matter, sweetie. It's not!" Tisha angrily retorted.

"Tisha, could you please tell me why your daddy still seems to be so concerned about us being together? I need to know. Why is he so worked up behind me being the one who's fucking you and not somebody else?" Melvin's way of how he phrased the question, seemed somewhat sarcastic.

"I do not know! He seems to not wanna give me a break when it comes to you," she replied.

"I thought you told me one time before that he liked me?" His sarcastic tone continued.

"He did. At least at one point."

"Well, he'll get over it. He needs to just face the facts. That's all there is to it. He gotta leave us alone. Like for real, he do."

"Maybe he will soon. But to be honest, I really don't wanna give it too much thought," she declared.

"He still got you holding money for him?"

"Yeah."

"Well then, there you go. As long as he still trusts you with his money... hell... trust you period, it ain't shit to worry about. He not gonna cut you off, sweetie. Your dad only trying to get you to leave me alone. But, my question is, he don't know anything about you and your cousin doing side deals together, do he?"

"Hell, I don't know! Maybe he do. Maybe he don't. All I know is that, I'm not gonna let none of his antics stop me from being with you, or stop us from doing business," Tisha let out.

Her intentions was to let Melvin know she wasn't going nowhere. "Also, I've got something for you too."

She then pulled her Chanel bag close and dipped her hand into it. She brought out a watch. The gift was offered to him. Melvin gladly accepted. It was a top dollar item. The price tag was $58,500. Melvin looked at the timepiece in awe. A big smile spread across his face. He took notice of the brand name. It was a red Ross Radiormir 1940 Oro Rosso.

Tisha spoke again. "Any nigga I make the choice to fuck with, I'm gonna make it a priority to be sure he gets nothing but the best. And I borrowed some of the money my daddy got me holding for him, so I could bless you with it, and be able to keep that smile on your face the long way, baby. Now, how real of a bitch is that?!" she proclaimed.

There was a serious look on her face. She leaned inward to kiss Melvin.

"Tisha! I don't think I heard you clearly. You did what?!" he had to ask. He wanted clarity on what he thought he heard her say.

"I said... I borrowed some of the money that I keep for my dad, so I can buy you an expensive gift. That's what I said. And I also made you an appointment for next week, to meet up with a tailor, so you can get measurements for this really nice silk suit I want you to have. I seen online. I liked it. It's made by Brooks Brothers. I want you to have a foot mold done too, for these handcrafted leather monk strap shoes by Di Bianco. They'll go well with the suit," she said, making him aware.

"What?!" Melvin let out. "Now, what if your dad finds out you took his money from him, Tisha? How you think he gonna take that?"

"My dad ain't gonna know jack shit about it. I got almost two million dollars of his money I'm holding. He always got me keeping his bread. And not one time do he even count it. I'm the one who does all that. So don't worry about nothing. I got this," she confidently said.

"Okay. Fine by me. And I thank you."

He eased closer to her. They began to tongue kiss. Although Melvin was not in agreement with her taking the money from her dad and spending it on him, he didn't say or do anything either, to stop her from doing so. He simply let it be. And be it was. The fact of the matter was that, Tisha fell in love with the man. And he in return, was now weak for her. It was a thrill of excitement to what they had. The relationship as a whole, was one the two wanted to make good on going forward into the future.

Tisha had shown and proved that she was worthy of the attention and the affection he gave her. The quality time they shared together, was the best. The only thing about it that caused them to feel a certain way, was the fact that they had to sneak around to be with each other. For two grown people, this was beneath them. Nevertheless, this was the reality of the situation.

Melvin would have to face Traci about his cheating on her in do time, adding more problems to his plate in the life he lived.

Chapter 4

MITCH began getting complaints from the youngest daughter—Chioma—about Tisha not handling business like she was supposed to with the salons like she had throughout times in the past. Chioma also complained to their dad that Tisha would often leave her two kids at her place, for her to look after them for many days throughout the week. But mostly on the weekends.

Chioma had two kids of her own to look after, although they loved being with their dad and their other young cousins on that side of the family.

Chioma knew everything about what Tisha and Melvin had. Tisha let her in on all of it. However, in return, Chioma got frustrated over the fact of no longer having any personal free time, because of have to keep Tisha's kids. She vented to their dad about these frustrations. Things got too stressful for Chioma. She found herself getting pissed at their daddy for him not doing anything about it.

One night, Mitch made it his business to make a pit stop by Tisha's house to confront her about it all. He wanted to check her for the old and the new. But, he wanted to be careful in a way, and not speak too much about the issues Chioma brought to him. There was no need to have them not getting along with each other.

The time was approaching eleven p.m. The idea was to show up late so to catch Melvin there, possibly. Mitch had no luck with this.

Once entering with a key he had of his own, he made his way directly to Tisha's bedroom to talk. The kids were in their rooms sound asleep.

"Tisha. Hey, baby. How you doing?" he greeted.

Tisha was sitting on the bed, watching a TV program.

"Hey. I'm fine, Daddy. What brings you by so late?"

Mitch sat down on the foot of her bed and took that opportunity to jump straight into things. "I thought I told you to leave that Melvin nigga alone. Why you seem to not listen to me?" he said.

"Daddy! What you talking about? And why you bringing something like this to me at this time of night?"

"What I'm talking about? I'm saying, you still dealing with Raymond's puppet? That's what I'm talking about." His tone got angry. Sinister even. "I got people pulling up on me right and left, telling me things. And I don't believe that they lying to me. What reason do they got to lie to me?" Mitch's voice and facial expression showed he was not in the mood for any lies from her.

"Well, Daddy, I got news for you. Whoever it is that's telling you anything, telling lies. And why you so bitter towards Melvin? That man ain't done nothing to you to make you feel this way about him."

Tisha sat up on the edge of her bed, ready to defend her relationship.

She continued, "It's Ray that you got the problem with. Not Melvin, Daddy." She made sure at this moment to lock eyes with him, showing no fear. She wanted him to know she was serious.

"No! You got that shit all wrong! I got beef with Melvin too! Because that low down, sorry nigga, gave me his word on something, then he changed it up on me. And in my line of work—in the lifestyle we live—all you have is your word. And once we shake on an agreement, that seals the deal. Ain't no turning around and backing out after you knew what the deal was. That nigga didn't even have the decency to at least be straight up like a man and face me. Instead, he took the bitch way out. That's my beef with that clown, even though I know for a fact, he a stool pigeon for Ray." Mitch's words were a little louder than before. But his eyes held a look of empathy and disappointment.

"So, Daddy, you mean to tell me is, all you want, is for Melvin to tell you straight to your face, that Raymond made him a better offer, and that's why he sided with him over you? That's all you asking from Melvin?" Tisha's words left him lingering in her thoughts.

"So, you mean to tell me that, for you to know all you do about Melvin, and whatever it is y'all got going on, is far more important than anything else? That this shit has gotten deeper than I expected?"

Tisha paused for a moment, thinking of what to say and how she was going to just be honest and say it. But she knew how her dad was going to react.

"Yes, Daddy. What we got is way deeper than you know. And Daddy, to be honest, we never took a break from dealing with each other like you told me to stop doing. We just hid it better from you. Us leaving each other alone will never happen. Because I love him. And he loves me. So, you just gonna have to deal with it." Tisha's tone was defiant and cold.

"So, you never took a break, huh? And I assume... it's what... just fuck me and all I said, huh?! Just forget about the fact he and Ray played me out of the club and out of my money, right? Basically, he shitted on me like I ain't shit. And you want me to just forget the fact Ray is using Melvin to spy on me, by Melvin using you," he spoke. He became angrier, thinking about how he was double crossed and betrayed. "Tisha, ain't no muthafucka' way, I can sit back and let a daughter of mine be involved with the enemy. Ain't no way." Mitch's voice dripped with more anger.

"Well, you gonna have to get used to Melvin being my man, Daddy. I love him and he ain't going nowhere no time soon," she said with a slight smirk, as she finally felt some relief that the truth was out.

She slowly rose up from the bed to her feet and faced her father with her truth. "And I wanna let you know something. And you hearing it straight from me first. I'm pregnant with the man's baby."

Mitch rose up quickly from the edge of the bed. He looked at his daughter sternly and was instantly filled with disappointment. He was overcome with disbelief and rage. Mitch became unbelievably pissed.

She continued before her father could respond to the bombshell she'd just dropped.

"And so you know too, I borrowed some of your money from the money I been keeping for you. I wanted to buy Melvin a few nice things. I'll be sure to pay you back in due time," she said with a smirk, as if she had won a chess match.

"Tisha, you did what?! You mean to tell me that you let that nigga get you pregnant, and, steal from me, all at the same time?! This for a nigga you know I hate?! Tisha! You done lost your goddamn mind! You gone crazy! How much of my muthafuckin' money did you steal?! Yeah, you stole it, because you sure as hell didn't ask me for it. So, how much?!" Mitch couldn't hold back his anger.

"I borrowed a hundred thousand, but I—"

"You ain't borrowed shit! You took a hundred thousand dollars from me?! Tisha!!! Look at me, girl. What-the-fuck has gotten into you?! What's your problem?" He demanded an answer.

"I said I'll pay you back, Daddy. Damn! My businesses together, will make a hundred thousand in ninety days or less. I'mma pay you back thirty grand a month until it's all paid back. I did it this way, because I knew you would have a problem with it. Daddy, you not the easiest person to ask for money. You don't know how to let things go. And, since I'm putting everything out there now, Melvin and I got an apartment. We live together. I'm not gonna tell you where it at, because I don't need you pulling up at our place and acting immature whenever you feel like it. You don't need to make a scene at our place."

"Stop! Just stop right now, goddammit! I believe I done heard enough. Come on," Mitch said, grabbing his daughter by the arm. "Come on now. Let's go. I want the rest of my muthafuckin' money out the safe now! Before this nigga brainwashes yo dumb-ass into stealing the rest."

He pulled her in the direction of the walk-in closet where the safe was. He slid the rack of clothes to the side to reveal a safe that was built into the wall. Tisha was made to punch in the passcode, and once it was opened, he began to stuff the remainder of his money into two pillowcases.

Tisha walked back over to the bed and plopped down on the edge of it. Her daddy was so mad, she didn't know what he would do next, so she was forced to listen to him throw threats at her and some of the nastiest words he'd ever said to her.

Once he got all of his money and finished telling her off, he began walking out the door.

But before he was all the way out the house, he said, "Okay, since you wanna play me like this over a nothin'-ass nigga, I tell you what. Don't call me for shit! Don't look for me to help you with shit no more! And don't expect me to change my mind either. Look to your man to do everything from here on out."

Mitch's words hurt her to hear, and hurt him to have to say. But what had to be don, had to be done, according to him.

Tears welled in his eyes. He was truly hurt that it had come to this. His own daughter betrayed him. She let the enemy come between them. Mitch was hurt but more so angry than anything. He had ill intentions on how to deal with his daughter and the Melvin's situation.

Mitch made it back to his truck. He grumbled to himself as he stuffed the pillowcases filled with cash in the back of the truck.

"She got some motherfuckin' nerve, don't she? How she gonna take money from me?! I mean, not even say a word until now. Then had the fuckin' nerve to tell me after the fact. That's stealing! Oh, she's lost her mind. Stealing from me for a no-good ass nigga!" he murmured to himself. He slammed the truck's back door then got in the driver's seat and started it

"I got something for that nigga though! Oh, yeah, I do," he spoke more to himself as he sped off.

Chapter 5

Days Later...

AFTER the fall out with her dad, Tisha felt the need to let Melvin know about it. They were at their apartment duplex.

"Baby, I finally had the courage to stand up to my daddy and tell him about himself," she began.

"Oh, you did? I'm proud of you. But what do you mean by that?" he asked.

"I told him everything," she said.

"That don't explain nothing to me. What is everything?" he asked a little more sternly this time.

"I told him everything. Even some things I haven't even told you yet." she smiled.

"What did you say?"

"Well, how about, he came into my house unannounced close to midnight. He tried to check me again about my dealings with you. He said something about he had other people approaching him, telling him they seen you and me out and about together."

"That's definitely a lie there, because we ain't been out nowhere in public together in Miami," he responded.

"I know, right. But anyway, he went on and on about how he feels about me and you being together. He don't want me to be with you or with anybody that's friends with his enemies, as he put it. He threw all kinds of bullshit at me." She took a pause then started back. "That was the point. I had had enough! I told him all I thought and how I felt. That he needs to fall the fuck back from you. And you not going nowhere out of my life. And he needs to get used to you being in my life. Because we gonna be together regardless of whoever or whatever," Tisha said.

"You told yo daddy all that shit?" Melvin asked, because he was surprised by it all.

"Hell yeah, I did. He's wrong about you and everything. I had to let him know. I told him about the money I got out of the stash and all. He was mad."

"I know you gotta be bullshittin' about that too, right?!"

"No! I'm not. But here is the part that he seemed to hate the most." She took a pause to brace herself for the reaction that Melvin was going to respond with. "I told my daddy, that I'm pregnant. And the baby is yours."

Melvin sat on the bed speechless. He simply looked at her with a strong contact of the eyes.

"Did you hear what I just said? I'm pregnant, Melvin. This why I took the money from my dad and bought you those gifts with it. And I wanted to tell you sooner. But I felt the need to wait until the right time. Obviously, the right time is now."

Finally breaking free from his dumbfounded state of being, Melvin spoke up.

"Yeah, I heard you. I'm just busy tryna process everything. That's all," he said, leaning in to give her a kiss.

"I love you, Tisha. I mean that. From the very first time I laid eyes on you and said something to you, I knew in my heart that eventually, we were gonna get to this point." His words were spoken clearly and politely. He meant all that he said.

"I love you too, Melvin Tyrell Anderson. Always know that. Okay. And now, we can move forward from here. My dad took the rest of his money from me and told me he was done with me. He said I better never call him for anything again. He told me to go to you for my needs from there on out," she said.

"I ain't got no problem with that. No problem at all."

"Me either." Her response came as a bit of relief. "So, how's everything going with you and Mr. Ray, as you would put it?"

"Oh, that. Everything good. I'm supposed to be meeting up with him again at the house he owns in Palm Beach. That nigga really living, Tisha. He got some lady he fucks with living there. She looks like she in her early thirties," Melvin said. "But I know she's a little older."

"Ray got more women than he can handle."

"Now that, he does. She really cool though. She big time into the real estate thing. Very polished. Very sophisticated. And real classy in her ways. More than likely, I'mma have the chance to take you to meet her one day. I'm sure you two gonna get along perfectly fine."

"Really, Melvin," she let out in an insulted type of way. There was no way she could allow herself to connect with one of the mistresses of the man who was the prime enemy of her father. No matter how bad the fallout was between her and her dad, she wouldn't do that.

"Do you honestly believe I wanna meet with Ray?! Raymond Stephens?! And one of the bitches he got in his life?! Like for real, bruh!" she stated.

"Well, I work for the man now. So all that taking sides with ya daddy and shit, gotta go. Besides, the man already cut me a nice check. So the beef between him and ya daddy, ain't got shit to do with me. And on top of that, me and you, ain't got shit to do with any of their problems either. A'ight?" he declared for the record.

"Yeah, I guess you right about that. But anyway, we gotta get busy making plans and preparing to bring our baby into the world. So, all that bullshit with everything else for the birds and the bees," she let out, looking to have Melvin understand the reality of the situation in the way she did.

The two love birds continued with their conversation. Good sex followed, taking them well into the night. They were happy together with what they had. Relationship vows were taken. They swore to not let anything or anybody come between them. Especially no other females. She already assumed he had others, but never actually seen nobody else. But, Tisha knew nothing about Traci. She and him were good to go. They were ready for the world at large.

Two Weeks Later...

MITCH STILL FOUND himself in a salty mindset over Tisha and Melvin being together. He burned with fury about this. And with him now knowing that his daughter took money from him to buy Melvin gifts, this intensified the situation. Not only did he no longer want anything to do with Tisha, so long as she was with Melvin. He ordered the baby girl—Chioma—not to either. Or she too, would be cut off from the benefits he provided.

This dude was pissed beyond all reconciliation, and never really thought that his daughter would pick and choose sides against him with a dude that was down with his worst enemy. Your worst enemy was once your best friend. Also, at no time while keeping money for him, had Tisha ever took a dime. But, all that was out the door now. That $100,000 taken to buy gifts and to appease Melvin with, threw all trust out the window. She had truly gone too far. And her level of disrespect and violating she done, brought more problems. Melvin was able to move her in whatever way he saw fit

Mitch had bad intentions in the making, and looked to take aim at Mr. Raymond. Melvin now too. If he wasn't able to get to him, the idea was to rob and kill anybody who was related to him—Mr. Raymond—or who worked for him in the underworld. If this meant to kill the nigga's wife, his young teenage daughter, or that faggot-ass son of his, Ray Jr., so be it, thought Mitch. That's what I'll have done.

Little known facts about Mr. Raymond that most didn't know was that, his first-born, Raymond Eugene Stephens Jr., was full fledged homosexual. He loosely flaunted these ways and absorbed himself within the lifestyle. Raymond Jr., perceived himself as a female in all aspects of thinking. He went so far as to have cosmetic work done to himself to enhance feminine qualities of his body. He owned two houses. One was in the north in New York City, and the other, was out west in Napa Valley, California. Both of his houses were far and out the way from his father.

Hatred by the father was expressed through the years. Raymond Senior didn't like the way the boy turned out, and he would often on him at the onset. In times past, Mr. Raymond would often physically and verbally abuse his son, until one day, Mr. Raymond's sister intervened, and offered to take the boy into her home to finish raising him. She had no problem letting the boy live that type of lifestyle he chose to live. He was free from discrimination or anymore abuse.

Raymond Jr. was fourteen at the time he went to live with his aunt. Although Mr. Raymond had the money and the means to pay his son's way into college, any prestigious university in the country, or in the world for that matter as many assumed he would do, Raymond Jr., successfully earned a top scholarship to attend Dartmouth College. He earned a master's degree in political science, and his minor was in banking and account management.

Also, Ray Jr. went on to attend Columbia University before graduating and becoming an independent filmmaker. He was dual city based in New York and Los Angeles with his documentaries.

Raymond Jr. happened to meet his life partner there in New York City while at Columbia. He was in his early fifties and wealthy. A white male who was a high profile real estate developer there in New York. The two met at a popular gay club called Club Eclipse in the VIP section. They traveled the world together and visited cities where their lifestyle was accepted. But primarily, they lived and did things together mostly in the Golden State where they owned a vineyard and winery. Mr. Raymond had a heavy stake in the business with his son in this area.

Through the years, the father and son were finally able to reconcile their differences. The strain that long pinned down the relationship was removed. Raymond Sr., eventually apologized to his son for all the wrong he'd perpetrated against him. The son accepted and went on to forgive the father. They mended the broken bond and went on to do business together.

It was Ray Jr., who played a major role in his father's decision to get away from the club industry and establish a footing in the political realm. Even if that meant only on a municipal level.

Mind you, Raymond Jr., had a master's degree in political science. The father took the son's advice and paired this with the vision that his own father had for him on the back end of the equation.

Mitch knew everything. He knew Raymond's family well. He knew about Raymond's businesses on the top surface, and he knew how to get at Raymond and hit where he could do the most damage on the low end. And he wanted blood. Dude was determined to get it too. However he could. One way or another. He and his team already won a battle by tracking down one of Ray's top men, kidnapping, robbing, and beating him to the point of near death. The plan was to repeat the same strategy that was perpetrated against Big Mix. But not on the son, Ray Jr. This time, on Melvin, if the opportunity presented itself.

Mitch felt that Melvin was easier to get, since he was around Miami and also fucking his daughter. He got in touch with his nephew again, Roland, to let him know what the next move was to be. Roland made his way to Mitch's home, and he was let inside. Mitch didn't hesitate to jump straight into it.

"Nephew, I'm glad you could make it. I got a new set of problems that we need to deal with," Mitch stated.

"I'm glad to be here, Unc. And I know it ain't no problems you got that we can't get rid of."

"How about, that fuckin' cousin of yours Tisha, done lost her muthafuckin' mind!"

"Damn, uncle Mitch! What in the world she got going on?"

"My own damn daughter, done gone all the way off the grid, nephew!"

"Awe, man, Unc. What she do this time?"

"Her hot ass, so-called herself now sleeping with the enemy!" Mitch revealed.

Complete silence came between the two. Roland didn't know how to respond to the revelations about his uncle's daughter. And the best thing he could have done, was to keep quiet. This was what he did.

Mitch continued, "So, she calls herself fucking with some nigga that's close to the nigga I hate most now, Ray," he revealed.

"Huh! How's she gonna go off and do something like that and disrespect you in the process?" Roland remarked.

"That's not even the half of it, nephew. How about, that little no-good cunt, had the nerve, to steal money from me too! So she could buy this nigga gifts and shit. And, she pregnant by the nigga too! Now, ain't that a bitch!!! The lil ho, took $100,000 from me! From her own daddy."

"Please tell me you bullshittin', unc?! You gotta be kidding me, right. Tisha didn't do no shit like that, did she?! Not your daughter, Tisha."

"I bullshit you not, nephew! Tisha done lost her muthafuckin' mind! I was okay with her being with the nigga at first. Hell, I even offered him a position at my new spot once I get things up and poppin.' But the nigga chose to take sides with that nigga Raymond over me, after he agreed to be on my team. He later turned and sided with the enemy like I said, and took my daughter along for the ride. That nigga a bitch!!!"

"So, you somewhat know the nigga we now discussing?"

"Yeah, I know of him. He one of them chump ass niggaz who used to work at the club that me and Ray had. K.O.D. was the place he and Tisha met."

"Oh okay, I see where you going with this now. I see what the deal is. It's a possibility that the nigga, Raymond, could be using him to get to you through Tisha." Roland was able to put two and two together. He continued to instigate the situation.

"That's exactly my point, nephew. But Tisha... her dumb-ass... too goddamn stupid, to not be able to see that like you just did. And it didn't take you long for you to see the problem with that. The little bitch done really pissed me off, nephew," Mitch vented.

"I know she has. And I can see why you mad too. But fuck all that. What you need me to do?!" Roland asked with his trigger finger itching. He was ready to get busy.

"I need you to spy on them muthafuckas' for me. The little bitch claimed that the both of them got an apartment together, but never said where."

"Nah-nah-nah, Uncle Mitch. Fuck all that spy on them shit! Just go ahead and get busy like you know how to get busy. All you gotta do is creep over to that heifer's house one night and put that tracking device under her truck. Everything else gonna work itself out from there," Roland suggested.

"You make a good point, since the little bitch don't wanna tell me where she shacking up at with the nigga. So, we might as well let her dumb ass lead us straight to him. And once y'all find out the spot where they stay, at the first that opportunity presents itself, y'all rob and shoot the nigga right there on the spot! But, you already know y'all gotta go in, tie up both of them, because I don't want Tisha to know who y'all are—you and your crew—and do what y'all do. But, don't hurt Tisha. I want y'all to pistol whip that nigga and take everything they got. Then, y'all whack that pussy ass nigga! You hear me! I want him dead!" Mitch's dictation was fierce.

"I got you, Uncle Mitch. I got you. Say no mo," Roland replied.

The plan was now laid. They both went to work. The very next day, on a Sunday, instead of Mitch being the one to plant the tracking device under Tisha's ride, he had Roland to do the honors for him. Dude crept to her home in Little Haiti to do the work at hand.

Tisha's Range Rover was parked in the carport with the door to it left up. Roland had easy access inside the truck. He popped open the hood and properly connected the hot wire from the tracking device to the battery for prolonged life, due to Mitch giving him a spare key that he had to Tisha's automobile.

Before the day, Tisha would often let her father have the privilege to drive her truck about town, to take care of his business he needed to attend to. This was especially so during the times when those really expensive tune up services were due. Mitch would take care of the tab for his her with no problem. On one of these service visits, he got a step ahead and had a spare key made, just in case of emergencies. As it turned out, his prediction proved to be beneficial. At least in this instance.

Roland thoroughly situated the device beneath the truck and was sure it was connected and activated, then moved on about his way without making the slightest amount of disturbing noise.

All that was left to do next was to keep tabs of the truck's movement through the GPS associated with it. They were in business.

Chapter 6

TISHA didn't have any idea that she was being tracked by her dad and cousin through the system of the device. Melvin didn't either. At any given time, he would be along for the ride with Tisha whenever they toured Miami or rode about to other cities together. Anytime Mitch or Roland checked the movement of her's, they knew the whereabouts of Tisha.

Notes were taken of each address and location the truck made a stop. Melvin's mother's home address was taken note of too. He'd taken Tisha by there to introduce the two of them one day. The intention was to make Mrs. Irene aware of the fact that they had a baby on the way. Her second grandchild.

All the information that was taken by Roland, he stored it away into an e-mail account, to be used when the time was at hand. He and Mitch had access to the account together.

Throughout the waiting process Mitch and Roland went through, sitting tight for something of importance to develop, they learned that Tisha's truck would have prolonged stays on most weekends and on certain nights throughout the week at a location in South Miami Heights.

To know for sure what was up, Roland took the drive to the location one night to see for himself. Indeed, this had to be the duplex apartment where his cousin and the dude lay up together. Tisha's truck wasn't immediately noticed. Not until after the fact. Roland parked down the road and walk back to the apartment, taking cover in the patch of bushes nearby. He then strolled around the place, now looking at the vehicle there situated in the back of the rest haven.

So, this is where your little sneaky ass been ducked off at lately, huh! You and that nigga of yours your daddy don't like, Roland thought to himself. "Uncle Mitch gonna love this information I got for him now."

Roland made the drive back to the inner city, He called Mitch to report what he now knew.

"Uncle Mitch, I got know where they been shacking up at, now," he revealed.

"Oh yeah?! Boy, you good, ain't you, nephew! So, where they been laid up at?" Mitch responded.

"At a duplex down in South Miami Heights. I almost missed it at first, because Tisha keeps her truck parked behind the place, maybe to keep people from knowing. But I crept up to the back of the place to know for sure that it was the spot," Roland said with excitement.

"I like the way you get down, nephew. To the bottom of the situation. I really do. And it's still plenty of time in the night before the sun comes up. So, this what I want you to do. Round up your boys and y'all get ready to handle that business for me, okay. Tonight, seems to be a good time to run down on him while we got him isolated in one spot. It ain't no telling when we may get that chance to catch him down bad again. And I don't wanna miss this opportunity. We gotta take it now! Another time may not come," Mitch spat as he gave the order for them to take action immediately. Melvin was a prime target in the cross hairs.

"No problem. I'm on it. I'm about to hit up my niggaz now and let them know to suit up. We got work to do tonight. And since that last lick you set us up on turned out well, I already know that these niggaz gonna be eager to do anything, whenever we get a call from you about something. But look, I'mma hit you back later, once we take care of the business," Roland said.

"That's a bet, nephew. I'mma be up and waiting on you to call. I'm out," Mitch lastly said then killed the call.

Roland got busy calling up his two most trusted goons, Flex and Bone. These two here, were money hungry and crazy enough to do just about anything to get it. The root of all evil had the power to control them however it willed.

The goon trio—Roland, Flex, and Bone—were all suited and booted and strapped to the hilt with firepower to take down Melvin. They had the leeway to rob him for whatever he had, and then, whack him then and there on the spot.

The plan was to pull a hardcore home invasion. They would break their way in, handle the situation, then ease out, the same way they came in. Only with Melvin dead from that point. They jumped to the occasion and took action.

Boom!

The back door to the apartment was crashed in by a large foot. It belonged to the most brutal of the three, Big Flex. He stood at six-eight and weighed 300 hundred pounds. The door came clean off the hinges with that one tremendous blow.

At that moment, the intruders made their way in. Melvin and Tisha were situated in the bed, watching an episode of The Sopranos on HBO MAX. Melvin was eager to catch up on all the episodes he'd missed while he was locked away. The two hadn't long finished making love. Tisha was still naked and asleep, and Melvin, had on his boxers and nothing else.

Startled like never before, Melvin immediately reacted on instincts, pushing Tisha from the bed to the floor and then getting down beside her. He grabbed the Ruger pistol of his that had a full clip at the ready. The moment a target was to present itself, he was going to blast. He took the remote and turned off the TV. This happened just in time to block out the lighting in the room and prevent the intruders from spotting them so easily.

The intruders reached the door of the bedroom where the couple were ducked off next to the bed. The door to the space was already halfway open when the lead goon, Roland himself, kicked it open farther. He was met by Tisha yelling out loud in fear.

"Ah!!! no!!!"

Melvin wrapped his hand around her mouth to muzzle her, as Roland waved his pistol from right to left, looking to lay his eyes on anyone. The beam from the infrared laser attached to the firearm sliced cleanly through the air. Melvin swiftly raised up from the opposite side of the bed and began blasting away.

Pop-pop-pop-pop!

The intruders returned shots.

Pow-pow-pow!

Boc-Boc-Boc!

While Melvin was taking his shots, he notice that the intruder who was in the front, began to slowly slump to the floor. Apparently, he'd hit one of them. He got to his feet and began stepping forward in the direction where the remaining two intruders now backpedaled. He fired away at them.

Pop-pop-pop-pop-Pop!

A full-blown gun battle was now going down. One of the attackers had an assault rifle and put it to work.

Tick-tick-tick....

The AR15 Bushmaster had effectively caused Melvin to now backpedal himself and re-position himself next to the bed to protect his pregnant girlfriend. Tisha began to shout again from her position on the floor. Her screams were to the top of her lungs.

"Tisha, shut the fuck up!" Melvin said to her through clenched teeth.

Tip-Tip-Tip-Tip-Tip....

The shooter with the AR-15 let loose with more rounds. He moved forward to the doorway of the room. Again, his vision was impaired from the flashes that expelled from the barrel of the rifle. He strained to see.

Now, Melvin lifted again and blasted back.

Pop-Pop-Pop-Pop!

He dropped low once more. The big fella who was cutting loose with the AR, was struck in the shoulder by one of Melvin's hollow points. He was forced to back away and retreat, yet still blasted away with the rifle like he was Rambo in First Blood. He continued to dump out most of the rounds from the one-hundred-unit clip.

Tat-Tat-Tat-Tat-Tat-Tat!

Melvin was overwhelmed by the firepower that he faced from the OPS. However, all the shots he fired, he seemed to miss Melvin and Tisha completely. The damage to the strong shoulder of the AR toting menace was the reason for the misfires.

Melvin quickly jumped to his feet and let off more rounds before making a break for the window.

Pop-Pop-Pop-Pop!

He drove through the glass, shattering it in entirety as he did so, and landed on his shoulder to the ground alongside the duplex. Melvin raised up and continued to shoot through the window where the attacker previously stood. The remaining two were running in the opposite direction while being shot at.

Instead of using the way that they barged into the house, they ran out of the front door making their exit, desperate to get to the getaway car that they had parked at a distance from the duplex. Once they reached it, they got in and hauled ass, leaving behind a fallen soldier of theirs inside the apartment.

Melvin managed to kill one of them. He and Tisha didn't suffer any gunshot wounds themselves through the entire shootout.

Chapter 7

MELVIN speed walked away from the apartment, putting distance between himself and the sight of the shootout. He only had on his boxer shorts, nothing more. He had no phone and his pistol in one hand. Surprisingly, he still had his watch phone strapped to his wrist. He would often sleep with it, a habit he picked up while in prison, to prevent him from missing breakfast early in the morning once chow call was announced

He took notice of the communication device in his arm. Once the rush of adrenaline was no more, he hid in a thicket of bushes nearby. He ducked low within and was intent on making a call. Melvin was about a football field away at a distance from the duplex. There was a desperate need to reach Tisha so to know that she was unharmed throughout the deadly barrage of slugs that was exchanged.

Back inside the apartment, Tisha was still curled up on the side of the bed, crying, panicking, and terrified out of her mind when her cell phone rang. She and Melvin both had iPhones with smart watches. The phone lit up on top of the nightstand on the opposite side of the room where she was positioned. Unknowing if the attackers were still in the place or not, she didn't make a move, letting the phone go to voicemail. Melvin called again. Tisha knew it had to be him, with the quickly repeated calls, but wondered why he had not came back to safeguard her. Finally, she dove across the bed to grab a hold of the phone, taking note of Melvin's phone as well.

If his phone's here, how the fuck is he calling? she questioned. "Hello! Please tell me this you, Melvin?!"

"Tisha! Can you hear me? You hear me right?! Yeah, it's me. Can you hear me good?" he asked frantically.

Hysterical and at the brink of having a panic attack, she answered him twice over. "Yes, I can hear you! Yes, I can hear you, baby!"

"Okay, good. Calm down and listen to me."

"Where you at?!" she chimed in on instinct to ask.

"I'm just down the road. But listen, okay? Get my phone and get the fuck up outta there now! But be sure to grab my phone and get out of there now while I'm talking to you," he stated. He wanted her to move swiftly before the cops were to show up.

"Okay, baby. Okay. I'm doing it now,", she responded. "How was you able to call, baby?"

"I got my watch phone on, babe." She got up then began to make an exit out the room, but frozen in her movements.

"Ahh! What the fuck?!" she shouted.

"Baby, what's wrong now?" he asked. His blood began to boil through his body once again.

"It's a dead guy in the doorway of the room. Baby, it's one of the people who broke in and shot at us. He got a mask on," she shouted.

"Tisha, don't touch him. Just get my phone and get your keys and get the fuck up outta there," Melvin demanded.

"Okay-okay, baby. I'm going."

"And be sure to turn out the lights in the place before you leave, sweetie."

The dead man was laid sprawled out, facing upward. Tisha stepped over him and exited the apartment. Melvin was still on the phone.

"When you leave the driveway, baby, go to your right. I'm here down the road."

"I'm on my way to get you now, baby." She assured him then she got into the truck, fired it up, and pulled off, en route to pick him up. "Where you at, baby? I don't see you."

"I'm looking at you now coming down the road," he said in reply. "Slow down," he let out now.

Appearing from the hiding space where he was located, he hopped inside, and they rode away. Melvin grabbed hold of his phone and immediately called his cousin, Vick. The time was late. Vick didn't immediately answer. Melvin called back a second time. He had success now.

"Yo, what up, fam? It's almost three in the morn—"

Melvin cut him off mid-sentence.

"Yo, cuz! Where you at, nigga?! I got a serious situation on hand, fam!" he revealed with a state of panic in his voice.

"Calm down, nigga. What the fuck going on? And apparently, it must be over with, since you on the phone with me now. But what's going on?" Vick asked with a grave concern in his voice.

"It was somebody who broke in on me and tried to kill me, cuz! But where you at now? We need to meet now, fam."

"I'm at Lulu's spot. Meet me here."

"I'll be there in twenty minutes. I'm coming from South Miami Heights."

"I'm here," stated Vick. He then ended the call with the last words.

Melvin turned to Tisha again. "Listen, when you drop me off, go straight to your dad's house, Tisha. Don't call the police for nothing, okay? Do-not, call the police! Okay Tisha! I mean that shit! And when you get to where your dad's at, tell him exactly what happened. Give him the location of the apartment. And I'm sure he'll know what to do from that point. Tell him about the dead nigga who still there and all. Mitch is a G at this type of shit. He'll know how to handle everything. Especially by you being involved in it. And I hope none of the neighbors didn't call the cops either.

But if they did, they may not know where the shots came from, since everything happened inside the spot."

"Baby, why you leaving me to do everything by myself?" asked Tisha.

"I ain't leaving you to do everything by yourself. I just told you to go to your dad. That he knows what to do in a situation like this. Also, we don't need the police involved. Because of who you are, and who I am, with my record and all. Just trust what I'm telling you, sweetie. It's all for the better. I'm still shook anyway, and I'm not thinking straight to make any decisions right now. So, just trust in what I say about your dad," Melvin stated to her. "And I would've thought you would've known all this by now about your old man. But I guess not."

Tisha didn't say anything to respond to all Melvin said.

Maybe her silence was an admission of guilt. Besides, Melvin did make a good point. All that her father was, everything he had going on, and the illegal business affairs he conducted, it should have been known to Tisha by now about all this. But apparently, it wasn't. The two reached the neighborhood where Vick's girlfriend lived.

"I love you, sweetie," Melvin said to her. Tisha locked eyes with him and kissed him. He got out of the truck, still only with boxer shorts on and his watch, nothing else, and quickly walked to the front door of the home where Vick awaited him. Melvin had texted once close by.

Tisha pulled away, headed to her father's house. As she drove, she called him to let him know that she was on the way. Unbeknownst to her, Mitch was already up. He was awaiting a call from his nephew, Roland. But instead, upon taking a look at the screen of his phone at the incoming call, he was taken totally by surprise, to know that it was his daughter. Mitch knew then that something must had not gone right with the special mission he'd sent Roland on. An eerie feeling developed in his gut. He prepared himself to hear the bad news.

"Hello! What's up, Tisha?! Something can't be right, because you calling me this damn late at night," Mitch said.

"Daddy! I'm on my way to you. To your house right now. I got an emergency. A serious situation happened. I'll tell you about it when I get there," Tisha let out.

"I'll be waiting for you when you get here," he responded and ended the call. Mitch then immediately called Roland's number, eager to hear from him. The call went to voicemail. He next checked to know the whereabouts of Tisha through the account linked to the tracking device. She wasn't too far away, maybe ten minutes or so at a distance. Mitch braced himself to hear what had happened.

Meanwhile...

BACK AT VICK'S girlfriend's house, Melvin was seated in the living room, now cloaked in a robe that Vick had given to him and letting his cousin know all about the incident that played out at the apartment.

"Fam! Me and one of my girls named Tisha were chilling in the spot. And nigga, next thing we knew, somebody bust in on us out of nowhere! I reacted with the quickness and pushed Tisha off the bed to the floor, then took over the situation. I grabbed one of my pieces, cocked it, and waited for a target to come in sight. I turned off the TV so it could be dark, and they wouldn't be able to see us that good. The door to the bedroom was already half open. The first nigga kicked it in. That was the point when I started blasting like crazy, cuz," Melvin related.

"What spot was you at? Which one you talking 'bout?" Vick asked, not knowing about the duplex he shared with Tisha.

"Me and Tisha got a spot together down in South Miami Heights. We been chilling there on and off for about a month now. We stay there maybe three to four days out the week. Sometimes less. Sometimes more."

"Okay. I got you now. But go ahead. Continue."

"So, anyway, when these fools finally do get in eyesight, I got busy first by blasting in their direction. The first nigga fired back at me. The nigga's gun goes upward to the ceiling. So I knew then that I had hit him. Next thing I know, the big nigga who was behind him, started to shoot. This nigga began gunning at me with a chopper or an AK or some shit like that. Something heavy! Because he let that bitch rip! And didn't seem to wanna stop!" Melvin said.

"So, how many was at you?"

"I don't really know exactly how many. But I do know there were at least two. Anyway, I began to bust back at 'em between those chopper rounds, hoping to scare them out or to back them up enough, so I could get out of there and make a break. But the nigga with the chopper went ape shit on me! Blasting away and didn't stop. I know that that nigga had to have let off damn near sixty rounds. I was a little funked up about this and made a break for it out the window. I dove straight through that muthafucka.' That was how I was able to get out of there."

"Where the fuck was the female when all this shooting and shit was going on?" Vick asked.

"She was still laying low next to me. Next to the bed. I had to get the fuck up out of there, fam. The number one rule of nature is self-preservation. But thankfully, my quick thinking and gunning back at them niggaz took one of 'em out and pushed the others back onto their heels."

"I know that's right. Your instinct saved y'all."

"Hell yeah, they did. And when I was out of the line of fire, I ran a down the road and then called the chick I was with. She was still in the house."

"How you managed to grab your phone with all those bullets flying?" Vic asked the obvious out of curiosity.

"I didn't," Melvin said.

He was observant of Vic's body language as he explained how the call was made. "I had my watch phone. My iPhone watch," he revealed, tapping the timepiece with two fingers.

"What the fuck?!" Vick blurted out with a laugh.

Melvin smiled at the reaction.

"I picked up the habit while I was in prison, cuz. I needed to keep track of time and keep the alarm set early, so I wouldn't miss breakfast."

"Nigga, you crazy as hell, fam," Vick uttered with a smile. "That's logical thinking though. Strange, but useful."

"But anyway, as I was talking to her, she scrambled around the room, looking for my phone. Then she screamed like hell."

"For what?"

"She said it was a dead nigga. He was laid out in the doorway of the room. That's how I know I had killed one. He had on the ski mask, she said. I told her not to touch him and to hurry and get the fuck out of there. To come and pick me up. That I was down the road. This was what she did when I got in the truck with her. I grabbed my phone then called you at that point," stated Melvin.

"You didn't call the police, did you?"

"Hell-the-fuck-no! The fuck wrong with you, nigga!" Melvin replied emphatically. "I told the bitch to call her dad. He's an OG. He know exactly what to do. I also told her not to say shit to nobody but her dad, to let him handle everything. I don't need static from the police. Especially not about no goddamn homicide."

"That was a smart move, cuz. And you ain't sure if or not the neighbors called the police?"

"I don't think they did."

But if ol' girl dad the OG you made him out to be, to clean up the mess that you was involved in, when he does go to the spot to see what the deal is, he'll more than likely get rid of the body, right, right?"

"Right. Because he wouldn't want his daughter put in the bullshit by the police," Melvin injected.

"Exactly. One thing will lead to another. Then, before they know it, the police or the Feds would be investigating him too."

"Right. But look, Vick, all I know is that, I gotta get the fuck outta town, fam. And I'm talking ASAP! I got two problems to worry about now. The muthafuckin police. And, the family or the crew of the nigga that I popped. And I can't go back to prison, fam. That's an automatic twenty years for me, no matter how much to the letter of the law I followed. That stand your ground shit won't hold up under a possession of a firearm by a convicted felon while on probation and in the commission of a felony, is enough to have them crackas' busy trying to bury my Black-ass alive, and I'm not about to sit around and wait here in Miami for them to come get me either. I gotta go back up the way to New York, my nigga!"

"Hell yeah, cuz. You gotta get the fuck on. But you got any idea on who it was that sent them at you?"

"No. Not a clue. It could've been that nigga, Calvin. It could've been anybody I had a beef with. Hell, I don't know. But look, I'mma go ahead and call Mama and let her know you coming by to get a few things of mine. I got about seventy-five thousand in cash and an expensive watch there. My girl paid about sixty thousand for it. I got another pistol there too. Oh, and Ko-Ko there too, cuz. I'mma give her to you to keep for me for the time being, until I get situated up top. I'm a send for my bitch then. It shouldn't take too long for me to get situated, maybe about a month or two. But in between the time, I'll be back-and-forth there and here, to check in on Mama, and to report to the probation people. And you already know, big bro, he's still over there in that place, the asylum. You gotta be sure Mama have the chance to see him at least once a month, fam. I'll see to it that her aid—Porsche—continue to do her part and take care of

Momma wherever else she needs to go. Them two really cool. And our neighbor, Miss Sheila, she's been the one taking good care of Mom through the years I was gone. So for the most part, that's top priority there, fam," Melvin stated to his cousin.

"What about your truck?" Vick asked.

"You can ship it to me on the train later to, New York. Or, better yet, just drive it on your next trip there. My plan is to stay away as long as possible, until I know I'm not a wanted man. Until this shit blows over. I gotta call Traci too, and let her know what's up. I'mma get her to drive me to Jacksonville, so I can catch the train this afternoon that's headed north. Matter of fact, lemme call her ass now. Gimme a minute, cuz, okay?" Melvin said to Vick.

He called up the main girlfriend. She needed to know to be ready for a trip. To take him to north Florida later in the day.

Chapter 8

In The Meantime...

ACROSS town, Tisha finally made it to her father's house. The two sat in the living room of the mini mansion. Tisha related to the best of her ability everything that transpired with the home invasion gone wrong.

"Daddy, all I can remember, is hearing the back door being kicked down, the bedroom door busting open, and Melvin pushing me to the floor to keep me from being shot! When the first guy came in sight, that was when Melvin went to shooting," she stated.

"Did he hit the first guy?" asked Mitch.

"Yeah, he did."

"But how do you know if or not he killed the first guy?"

"Because, when it was all over with, Melvin made a breakout for it. He dived through the window. I had to get his phone for him and get out the apartment myself. The dead guy was in the doorway of the bedroom facing up. He had a ski mask on. I had to step over him to leave the room. He still there right now. Dead as shit!"

"What! So, where Melvin at now?"

"He had me to drop him off at one of his cousin's house. He was the one who told me to call you, not the police. Melvin I'm talking about. And he also said, you was an OG when it came to these type of situations, and you was better suited than he was, to handle something like this. He said he wasn't thinking straight enough to make rational decisions."

"Humph!" he scoffed. "I see he was able to think well enough in a tough situation. But anyway, I'm sure by now that your ass, gonna finally let me know where this apartment at y'all got, ain't you?" Mitch let out his words in a sarcastic way. He had a hard time keeping his composure and didn't reveal how pissed he really was. However, he maintained.

"Well, what's the address to this damn apartment y'all got?" he demanded to know.

Tisha gave him the location of the duplex. He stored it his cell phone.

"Now, take a good look at me." Mitch now had a serious mean-mug about his face to indicate how for real he wanted to be with her about all he was about to say. "Do not, I repeat, DO NOT, say anything about this shit to nobody! I mean, I don't want you to utter not one word to nobody! Period! Not your sister. Not your bestie. Not your cousins. Not to nobody. Do I make myself perfectly clear?!"

"Yes daddy. You do," she responded.

"I mean that shit, Tisha! Because if word gets out about this, your ass could go to jail! For a long fuckin' time! But look, gimme the key to the place. I'mma pass through there later to find out if or not somebody in the neighborhood had called the cops. And once I do that, I'mma go back a day or so after, get the dead body out of there, and get rid of it. But who name the place in?"

"Melvin paid some crackhead woman he knew to put everything in her name for us," she revealed.

"Good. Now we ain't gotta worry about the landlord putting the police on you once they see all those muthafuckin' bullet holes throughout the place," Mitch related. "Now, take your ass home and lay low out the way for a time being. I'll let you know when the coast clear to come out. And I know I told your ass before not to come back my way for nothing. Yet, here you are."

For some reason, maybe from anger, Mitch made it his business to throw this up in his daughter's face. Possibly out of spite.

"Come on, Daddy. This is a very serious situation," she responded.

"And stealing my motherfuckin' money to take care of another nigga, a very serious situation too! So, I got a right to feel the way I do now. Get the hell out of my damn house! I done heard enough of your shit for now. I'll be sure to call you when I'm ready to," Mitch lastly stated to his daughter, got to his feet, and pointed toward the front door.

Tisha stood herself, looked on at her dad with a face of disbelief, then slowly walked to the door to exit. They said nothing more to one another in the moment.

MELVIN MADE THE call to Traci. After several attempts, she reluctantly answered.

"Hello," she laid out; her voice had a bit of aggravation in it.

"Traci, it's me."

"Oh! It is?! So, you finally remembered you got a girlfriend, huh? After going for so long without me seeing you or hearing from you, it's obvious you need me for something. Because you calling at this hour. So what's up?!" Traci let out in response to Melvin.

"Traci, now ain't the time for all that, sweetie. Now, simply ain't the time. But look, you gotta work today or not?"

"Yeah, I go in at three. Why?"

"Because, I'mma need you to call in and take a day off. You gotta take me to Jacksonville. I got a serious situation. I can't speak about it right now. I'll tell you in due time. But I need you to take me to Jacksonville today, okay?"

She fired back on cue to what he had said.

"Melvin! What the hell is going on? And who I'm talking to right now, Melvin or that nigga Parlay at the moment?"

"Traci, I'mma say it again. Because I see you didn't get it. Now ain't the time, baby. Okay? All I can say is that, I got into it with somebody over some old. That's all I can tell you now. So, you gonna take me to Jacksonville or what? And I'll be able to explain everything to you while we on the way, if you gonna take me?" he said to her.

"Yeah, Melvin. I'mma take you. Dang," she responded.

"Okay, good. I'm on my way over now. I'll be there shortly."

"Okay. I'm here," Traci lastly said, bringing the call to an end.

She then turned to face someone she shared her bed with. It was Angel, a longtime friend and lesbian lover who she also worked with. They both were still in the nude, after a night of passionate sex.

"Angel, Melvin 'bout to come over for a minute, girl. I gotta get up and take this nigga to Jacksonville in a little while," Traci made her aware.

"He would be the type of dickhead to pop up out of nowhere and come to fuck up something good, wouldn't he," Angel responded. "But it's all good, girl. I understand. So long as you continue to give me the best of you and not him, we gonna be good," Angel further let out. She then leaned over. Her and Traci began to tongue kiss.

Angel made a trail of wet lip prints from Traci's neck down past her belly, and ending at the gateway of her honey-hole. Traci had a gold hoop earring piercing on her clit. It resembled a door knocker. Angel took a slow swipe upward with her tongue between Traci's legs. She was intent on getting up to get dressed and leave before Melvin made it there. The two ladies wanted to keep their private life just that, private. It wasn't for anybody to know. Not even Melvin.

"Be sure to call me when you on your way back down I-95, okay, boo?" Angel asked of Traci. The two tongue kissed yet again. Angel got dressed and was escorted to the front door of the home by Traci. They made small talk throughout their steps.

"And so you'll know, I need you to inform me of all that that nigga got going on too. Okay? That way, I know how to safeguard you," Angel stated.

"I will," Traci lastly said

THE HISTORY OF Traci and Angel was deep. It was filled with compassion. They met when Traci got on at the hospital. They court one another for months, until Traci gave in to Angel's persuasions. She turned Traci out. The friendship grew stronger. This was because they worked at the same place, and mostly in the same area, during the same hours throughout the week.

Angel was a year younger than Traci. Lower in position too, as an LPN. Traci considered these times building up as the unsure moments. Because she was merely curious, and nothing more. But when Melvin did finally make it home and began putting the dick on her, she called herself bisexual.

Angel had no problem playing second fiddle to Melvin in Traci's life, because she felt that eventually, he'd fuck up somewhere down the line. Or would go out to be with other females, leaving Traci deserted. The thought was there too, that he would use her, since Traci was a gullible bitch for him and free hearted about giving people her help. Angel found a sweet spot with Traci though, and took advantage of her kindness and generosity.

Traci had a brother. He was her one and only sibling. Dude was an NFL superstar. He blessed her with $250,000 at the end of each season. When he first got drafted, he put $2,000,000 in Traci's bank account. His contract for the first five years was $54,000,000. So much of it guaranteed to him.

And he blessed Traci. She in turn, took care of both, her boyfriend, and the girlfriend. She loved and adored Melvin and Angel.

VICK GAVE MELVIN clothes to put on until he was to make the drive to Melvin's mother's house and get everything he needed him to get. He took care of the first part of the mission. From there, he took Melvin to Traci's house. She was already prepared to make the drive to Jacksonville. She was waiting on him to arrive so they could immediately hit the road.

The lie Melvin told his momma was, he was still working at the club. He said the job required him to travel. This was what he told her when he made the call that morning to let her know Vick would be coming by. He also told her that Vick, would be coming by from time to time to help her with things while he was away. The mother wished him well and told him to keep praying and to stay strong.

Melvin and Traci made it to Jacksonville just in time for him to board the Amtrak train—the Northwest Corridor. This was the one particular train bound for all major points of the Northeast. He had $25,000 in cash, three sweatsuits to battle the brisk February weather, a backpack with personal hygiene products, and of course, his phone and watch devices to communicate with, watch movies, and to listen to his beloved hip hop music. Rick Ross, Lil Wayne, Jay-Z, and Kevin Gates, were his personal Mount Rushmore of hip hop.

He kissed Traci farewell, and assured her he'd be home sooner than she anticipated. The truth, however, was Melvin had no idea when he'd be able to return to Miami without having to look over his shoulder. His words to Traci was only to pacify her emotions, as she suffered from bouts of anxiety and depression. She'd lost many loved ones, and really loved Melvin. She didn't want to lose him too, as a victim of crime. Or, to the prison system again.

If Melvin would only take heed to things and listen to her, everything would begin to turn out for the better, as far as what they had was of a concern. He accepted some of her advice, but never all of it. Her desire was to get him to slow down just enough, so he would be able to see the clear picture.

Traci was a far different breed than the other females he was use to. Or the ones she had a feeling he was involved with. He knew this. And without a doubt, he knew that Traci was there for him too. There was no questions about it.

Chapter 9

MITCH and the low-key bodyguard he kept close to him now, made the drive to the apartment. This was two days after the fact. He needed to find out exactly what the situation was. He had strong reason to believe that the nephew—Roland—was the one who was hit and lay dead there. Roland never called back to let him know what all went down. He never answered his phone any more when Mitch tried to call him. And, he never showed back up in person for Mitch to know if he was still alive and not killed in the melee.

Roland's two partners in crime, Bone and Flex, made no attempts to get in touch with Mitch either. If only they knew how deep in shit they were. This was due to them going into hiding. They now had three serious reasons why this was a must, to hide. One; they feared that the police was called. Two; they thought that maybe Melvin had found out who they were, and was now aiming to track them down to kill them. And three; they had a serious reason to fear that Mitch marked them for death, because they left Roland dead in the apartment, and they failed to get the job done.

The two also was aware that Mitch and Roland's brother, Haitian Vino, wouldn't have no understanding about nothing, if they came back to them with a dead Roland. So, either way, the two were destined to be whacked themselves. And they knew this. So, the best thing they could do, was exactly what they were doing: hiding.

Mitch parked his truck behind the place. They both got out. He instantly noticed the broken window that Tisha told him Melvin dove through. Mitch and the bodyguard went in through what was left of the backdoor. There was heavy damage.

"Brace yourself for what we 'bout to see," Mitch cautioned. When reaching the short hallway that led to the bedroom, they notice the damage left behind from the gun battle that took place. The vicious work of art was dotted all over the place. There were bullets holes everywhere. Mostly from the AR15 the intruders had.

"Yo, bro," Mitch let out. "Put on your gloves and go check the other areas for me. Be sure all the blinds and curtains closed," he further instructed. The space was lit enough from the light of day for them to see. The bodyguard went one way and Mitch the other.

Mitch looked down at the body that lay dead in the doorway to the bedroom. He knew it was Roland. The figure of the corpse made the indication. Not to mention the solid black high top Gucci sneakers on the feet of the person who was no more. He'd seen Roland with those on more than a couple times, and knew they were his favorite to step out in. Mitch kneel lower over the body and removed the blood-soaked ski mask, taking note that indeed, it was Roland.

He began to chant something of a prayer in their native Haitian-Creole tongue. Roland got hit in the forehead and the chest.

Mitch's bodyguard was back in his presence. He approached, taking notice himself of who the dead man was. The hired henchman fixed his face in a perplexed way and didn't utter a word while Mitch prayed and grieved the loss. Mitch brought everything necessary to retrieve the body.

He thought over how best to go about doing things over the past two days. The conclusion he came to was that, the most reasonable thing to do, was to simply dispose of the body without anyone knowing a thing. Not even the family.

This was because, if word got out, the family may have an ax to grind with Mitch, behind him sending Roland on a mission that led to him killed. Also, Tisha would then know that her dad was spying on her, and tried to have her robbed and killed too. Because she took his money, and was continuing to deal with Melvin, after he ordered her to leave that man alone.

Mitch's other conclusion, was to put a contract on Bone and Flex, and have them tracked down and murdered. Melvin too. All of this would be long after he and the bodyguard got rid of Roland's body. Mitch figured that if he or the hired hitter he was to put on the job, wouldn't be able to get a grip on the slippery fish that Melvin proved to be, he'd simply have his mother knocked off in his place, since he now knew where she lived. Tisha let it slip that she met the lady before. And Mitch definitely had a good idea how his daughter thought and how she moved.

Mitch felt strongly that Melvin may avoid Tisha for a time being, and wouldn't contact her until he knew what there was to know. If this was to be, Tisha would act out of frustration and impulse, get impatient, and make it her business to find Melvin herself, or at least try to. She would then start making frequent trips to the man's mother's house, looking to lay eyes on him. All Mitch had to do from that point, was keep tabs on Tisha through the tracking device underneath her car that she knew nothing about. This would lead Mitch and his hired killer directly to Melvin. And if not him, his mother.

In Mitch's mind, somebody had to die! That being either Melvin or his momma! He had other plans for Tisha and how he was intending to make her suffer behind her blatant acts of betrayal.

Tisha should have known better than to go against me! he thought. And at this point, things had gone too far.

Mitch and the bodyguard picked up the body, wrapped him in plastic and blankets, and finally loaded him in the back of the SUV. The bodyguard was to dropped off at home.

Mitch wanted no one other than himself to know the location where he was intent on burying Roland. The sun had set. Darkness was upon the sky. Roland's death would be quiet as kept.

Two Weeks Later...

MELVIN SETTLED WELL in Harlem, New York. He was staying between Yvette's place and the hotel suite he checked into. This was to be until Yvette was approved for an apartment she was in the process of putting in her name for him. Throughout the time, he had no contact with Tisha. In fact, he made it a priority to have all of his contact information changed. When the time was right and he had come to know what all he was trying to know, he would reach out to her then. But that wouldn't be anytime soon.

For the most part, he really didn't want anything to do with Tisha. Not until she had the baby, and he got down to the bottom of the chaos that took place. He was hellbent on knowing who was behind the failed hit. But, he only wanted contacted to his mother, Traci, Vick, and Mr. Raymond. Nobody else.

Eventually, he got in touch with Mr. Raymond, to let him know about the situation. Melvin gave the street veteran the real story. Also, the suspicion he had about who might it been. Mr. Raymond gave him solid advice and vowed to stay by his side to see him through the storm. Melvin was also given the word that no matter what, he still had a position with him.

Mr. Raymond also let Melvin know that he was having a dinner party reception to make his official announcement about his campaign bid to become mayor of Miami. And that if it was to be possible, he'd like for him to be present to be a part of it. But first thing was first: resolve the situation.

Melvin let Mr. Raymond know that he'd be there, and was more than honored to share the moment with him. He planned to do all in his ability to make it there to the event. Mr. Raymond wished him well and told him to be sure to keep in touch.

Calculated Measures...

AS MITCH PREDICTED his daughter would do, she began to make random stops at an address in the Brown sub section of town. Apparently, this had to be where Melvin's mom lived, Mitch reasoned. This was the one place Mitch knew she may be able to roll up on Melvin unexpectedly. Like as before, Tisha was tracked by GPS. Mitch wanted to be certain that the house Tisha stopped at was indeed Melvin's mother's. It had to be, because she made it her business to go by at least four times a week.

There was a police officer Mitch knew. He had him on the payroll. The cop was additionally paid to run a check on Melvin's driver's license. Mitch still had Melvin's application he filled out for the job—the one from the club, and the one from the premature agreement that they had. Sure enough, the residence on file for Melvin, had matched the one Tisha stopped by.

A designated killer was then hired. He had the duty to go and bump off the old lady, since the son wasn't available. At all cost, Mitch wanted to serve a sweet dish of revenge. This became the point when Melvin's mother was to meet a horrific death. All behind what her son had going on. The hitter disguised himself as an insurance salesman and went in to do work.

Chapter 10

Across Town...

THE aspirant and politically intoxicated Raymond Eugene Stephens, had formed a campaign team. They had the duty to move him along the way to become the next mayor of Miami, and to make him a hometown hero. A dinner party reception was formulated by yours truly, and was to be held at one of the local more exclusive country clubs and golf course resorts that Dade County, Miami, Florida had to offer.

The event was held at the Miami Shores Country Club on Biscayne Boulevard. There were many people invited. Dignitaries and various pillars of the community, to name a few. And of course, family and friends. The moment to make the big announcement was upon Mr. Raymond. He had his wife, Christine, who was there by his side. So was his teenage daughter, Erin. Also, there was Raymond Jr. and his partner, Sherman, to accompany him. Mr. Raymond's two brothers, Jeffrey and Gordon, their sister, Cora, and her two daughters, Donna and Estelle, were there also. Emanuel was certainly present. He had his wife and son to join him.

Mr. Raymond's legal team was on hand to share in the occasion. As crazy as it may be, Mr. Raymond had the audacity to have both his mistresses there to witness him initiate a career into politics. Camille and Felicia sat side by side and looked on in awe at their guy work his mojo. The personal bartender, Phaedra, was invited too, as Mr.

Raymond only trusted her to make his drinks for him. And finally, there stood Willie, the lone bodyguard that had a duty to protect the life of Mr. Raymond and his family. He'd done so for many years.

This speechwriter Mr. Raymond hired, drafted a well thought out manuscript for him to follow. And at the same time, he left plenty of room for Mr. Raymond to journey off script, the very thing he planned to do.

Mr. Raymond opened cordially. "Hear ye, hear ye!" he declared, taking to the stage and positioning himself behind the podium. He clanged a fine piece of silverware against the wine glass he drank from. It was a fork. Everyone present gave their undivided attention, and he proceeded.

"Greetings, my dearly beloved people who are gathered here today. As you all are aware, the reason we are here today, is to have you all come together as one, and support and promote yours truly, along the campaign trail. I'm in the hopes that I become successful and win the chair to the office I seek. Today is the day that we make it official that I, Raymond Eugene Stephens, is to hereby declare, that I am determined to be your next mayor of Miami," he stated. The crowd erupted in applause.

Mr. Raymond continued, "As far back as I can remember, my father, the late great Herman Stephens, instilled a vision within me as an inspiration. This was to be love and thrive upon. He said to me that the good Lord provided him with the vision indeed, one of his sons shall someday rise to the highest position and status that the city has to offer, and to this, one would lead and govern through the wisdom of God and rule of the law," he said. The crowd applauded once more.

"My father further stated to me that, his vision, not his dream, took place all throughout the night as he rested, and revealed many things. He made it priority to share them with me. He said that God related this from above, that this particular son, shall be blessed with many gifts, along with being charming and very handsome, wise, articulate, and shall gain a great measure of success!" The crowd clapped gleefully. The wife Christine, appeared to stand out with this more than others.

He continued, "My father also said that it was confirmed, that this son of his, who was destined to have the level of success that God had declared, would be the second born son. And that, my dear people, happens to be me, Ray-Ray Stephens. My father, went on to profess that the good Lord above, related that the second son, would additionally be two things: One; he would be a killer; and two, he would be a king! That is to say, my beautiful people, that he would be a killer of the competition, and, the king of the profession," Mr. Raymond proclaimed to the audience.

He kept going almost endlessly with the self-gratifying remarks that were purposely tied into the speech. Also, he thank and congratulated the ladies and the gentlemen alike.

As Mr. Raymond drew toward the end of the seemingly interminable speech, he began to conclude with remarkable comments he thought of, that had the potential to sit on the minds and the hearts of everyone who heard his words. What he said was this:

"Please, everyone, please. I encourage you. Listen to me and hear me well, will you?"

The undercover federal agents that were there were sure to tune in carefully and highlight this portion of the speech, as it was something crucial to what they were investigating with him, and, for what to be on the look out for later.

Mr. Raymond proceeded after a long pause. "What I am about to say now, goes out to my family, my friends, my colleagues, my enemies, and the Republican Party members who I now stand alongside, and to the sponsors. I want everyone to please know this much: The mayoral office for the city of Miami, Florida, Dade County... is no one else's to have... but mine! It's all for the taking! With that, I have finally stepped up to the plate, and have come to collect."

Between The Time...

WHILE UP IN New York City, Melvin made constant phone calls to his mom's home. Attempts were to no avail. This was done at least ten times in less than an hour. She never answered. Melvin knew his mother's schedule and had never known her to be out the house and away from the phone at this hour of the night. It was 8:00 p.m.

Damn! I wonder what the fuck mama got going on that's stopping her from picking up the phone? This ain't like her, he thought. He began to panic for a moment, unsure of what could be the situation.

Fuck! I hope everything's all good my mama down there. I need to hear from her, though, he further thought.

The next morning, time was nearing when he knew his mother would definitely be cooking breakfast and tuning in to her program to listen to with Bishop TD Jakes. Porsche wasn't on schedule to work this day. However, Melvin texted her, to ask if she could please make a stop by the house to check on his mother, to at least be sure that everything was okay with her.

"I can't at the moment," she replied, letting him know she wasn't available to do so, since she was out of town in Las Vegas on vacation with her sister.

The substitute nursing aide who was on-call in Porsche's place while she was away, had too many other priorities with patients to stop what she was doing and do so. So, it wasn't anything at the moment that Porsche could do to help.

Melvin next thought of who might be available to do so. Miss Sheila. Her name popped up in his mind. He thought to give her a call.

"Hello," she answered.

"Hey, Miss Sheila. It's me, Melvin," he responded.

"I know your voice. How you been? And what you been up to?"

"I been good. And I ain't been up to nothing too much. But listen, I'm calling you because I keep calling my mom's phone, and she not answering," he explained.

"I'm sure she's up by now, or at least she should be. Why in the world isn't that old lady picking up the phone? You must still be out of town or something?"

"Yeah, I am. I'm still out of town. I'll be back home in a few days though," he responded.

"But your mama probably had a long evening playing bingo over at the Lions Senior Citizen building, or over at the other place she and her partner in crime, Marjorie, been visiting lately," Miss Sheila revealed.

"Huh?! What other place?!" Melvin questioned with a serious tone in his voice. He was able to catch on to what it was Miss Sheila was implying.

"Melvin, listen please, son. And don't tell your mom I told you this, okay? But she been going over to the Arab store on 18th and 68th. Or over to the other one that's on 12th and 58th to play those coins machines they keep in the back." Ms. Sheila was technically snitching on Ms. Irene.

"My mama been doing what, Miss Sheila?!" he responded with a bit of shock in his voice. "And how long this mess been going on?" he wanted to know.

"About a year before you got out," Miss Sheila made him aware.

"So, my mama got a gambling habit now, huh?!"

"I'm afraid so, baby."

This caused Melvin to think over all the money he had his mother to keep for him while he was locked up. He had no idea if it was still there or all gone. Not once had he checked on it since being a free man.

"I got my bedroom shoes on now, Melvin. And I'mma go see for you what's going on. I'm on my way out the front door now while I got you on the phone."

"Thank you, Miss Sheila. I really appreciate it. Mama got me worried like crazy."

As Ms. Sheila made the walk from her front door towards Ms. Irene's, she continued to talk with Melvin. There was something in the tone of his voice she detected. Something of an impatient nature. Something related to karma even. This caused her to question him about it, if there was a problem on his end. And if or not he had reason to fear for the safety of his mother? She would know immediately what to do to help if this be the case.

"Melvin, it ain't none of my business or anything like that. But you ain't got yourself in any trouble that would effect your mama, did you?" She asked out of concern.

"No, Ms. Sheila. Why would you ask that?"

"I don't know. I'm just asking. I've been around a long time, Melvin. And I know what I know. Plus, your mama mentioned something to me about some people coming by the house not long ago, looking for you, and you don't ever seem to be around anymore to meet any of these people," she said. "It's like you running from something and she wanted me to keep an eye out on the house and on her whenever I'm not working Because you never know. There to do so," Miss Sheila made Melvin know of the particular concerns that his mother had vented to her.

"Nah, Miss Sheila. No recent troubles. It's just that, before I got locked up, I did have a few problems in the streets. And even though I let bygones be bygones, that doesn't mean that the people I had beef with done the same. And now that I'm home and been out around town, people see me again. And I don't know what might be on the mind of the next man," Melvin stated.

"I understand your point, Melvin. I really do. And I'm at your mama's front door now. Hold on for a minute, okay?" she said then began to knock on the door.

"Miss Irene. Miss Irene. You here, Miss Irene?" she called out. "Melvin, I hear the TV playing inside, but I don't see anybody." Miss Sheila then tried to turn the knob of the bar door. It was locked. The hitter had locked it behind himself when he left out.

"She's not here, Melvin. I'll come back again in an hour or so to check on her and let her know you trying to reach her, and to answer your phone call, okay?"

"Okay, Miss Sheila. Please do that for me. I'll call you back then. I know good and damn well that Mama should be up and going by then," Melvin stated.

"Okay, just call me back. I'll be here," she said then ended the call.

Melvin wasn't able to relax. He paced vehemently from the front of the hotel room where he was situated to the back and repeated many times. All types of ill thoughts passed through his mind. What could be going on or wrong with his mother? His gut feeling indicated something just wasn't right. And for him to be at ease and gain a peace of mind, he needed to hear his mother's voice. He had to be assured she wasn't in any harm's way.

Melvin decided to call Miss Sheila again. She noticed that it was his number.

"I'm here, Melvin," she answered.

"Any sign of her yet, Miss Sheila?" he asked.

"No, but I'm on my way back over there again. And I tried to call her when I got off the phone with you. I got no answer either. Hell, she's got me worried now," she expressed.

Once she was at Miss Irene's front door again, she knocked harder this time. The old lady still didn't appear to answer.

"Miss Irene. Miss Irene, goddamnit! You in there? It's me, Sheila," she called out, raising her voice a notch louder this time. "Still not getting an answer, Melvin," she said.

He became very concerned now.

"Fuck! I wonder what the hell my mama got going on that's keeping her from answering the phone or her door?"

"I can't even begin to say, Melvin. This definitely not like her. And I don't know what your mama could be doing or where she could be."

"Shelia, just please keep an eye out on the house for me. If anybody has stopped by or if anybody drops my mama off, you please be sure to let me know immediately. Call me, okay?"

"I'll be more than sure to do so. Melvin, this causing me to be worried probably just as much as you are. All these years I've been knowing your mama, I ain't never known her to do something like this before," Miss Sheila expressed.

"Me either, Miss Sheila. Just please call me if you spot her anytime today."

"Not a problem. I will. I'm off today anyway, so I'm gonna definitely be on the lookout. At that very moment I lay eyes on her, I'mma be dialing your number," Miss Sheila assured him.

"Thank you again, Miss Sheila. I really appreciate you," Melvin stated, then they ended the call.

Melvin was heading to the point of potentially losing his mind about his mother not picking up. He tried her number at least ten times more in a thirty second period. Still, he got no answer.

"Baby. You okay?" Yvette asked in an easy tone of voice. She took a seat next to him on the couch and began to rub on his back. It was clear to her by looking at him that something was going on terribly wrong. But what? She needed to know.

"Yeah, everything should be good. I'm good. I'm just busy trying to figure out why my mom not answering her phone. That's all," he said to her.

"Just try to relax, Melvin. Everything gonna be okay." Her words were spoken in a way to try and bring calm to his spirit. They were poetic even. She was a sensual and loving human being.

Chapter 11

THIRTY minutes later, Melvin got a text message from a strange number. He didn't know who it belonged to. Someone anonymous reached out to him. It read

SENDER: Yeah, you bitch ass nigga! I know damn well you didn't have the nerve to think I was gonna let you get away with killing one of mine and I don't kill one of yours, did you?! Now how do it feel to know that your mammy ain't here no more behind the fuck shit you done got caught up in? Let this be a warning to you, nigga! Don't fuck with the wrong nigga again!

Melvin sat with his back pressed against the chair and continued to look on the screen of his phone. He had a good idea who it was that sent the message. But l, if anything, how did Mitch get his phone number?

He thought, Well, if it isn't Mitch, then who is it? This was the part that baffled him and put him at a loss for words. But the text came through on the personal phone if his. The one that only family and Traci and Tisha had the number to. It never changed. The one to the business phone did, and then there was the phone that only had the contact to Mr. Raymond stored inside. It was a direct line of communication to him. Beginning the beat himself up over the reality of the situation, he continued to question things in his mind.

If that was the nigga, Mitch, and he know this much, what else do he know? And I hope that that nigga ain't did something to my mama?! Not my muthafuckin' mama! But that can't be, because he don't know where she live. And the only way he could've found out is through Tisha, and that better not be the fuckin case. That bitch better not have crossed me out! At that point, it really didn't matter how Mitch got the number. All Melvin found himself now concerned with was if or not Mitch had done anything to his mother, because she wasn't answering her phone, and he didn't know what was going on with her.

If this be the case, I need to get back at him some type of way.

Melvin figured that there was no need to keep calling his mother's phone and that he needed someone to simply go by the house and find out directly what the situation was. He didn't know if or not it was safe for him to go home and didn't want to risk anything. Another gun battle was subjected to take place if he did decide to go. Not to mention the issue behind him shooting the guy called Calvin Prescott and him not dying.

There was now two issues to deal with on two different levels. One, with the police if they had found who it was that shot the dude; then two, whether or not Calvin had found out that it was him who had shot him and was eager to retaliate. Either way, the situation just wasn't good for Melvin to go back to Miami. Not so soon anyway.

Melvin came to the conclusion that there was no need to call Miss Sheila back because what if Mitch did have his mother killed and she was found in the house by Ms. Sheila? There was no doubt about it. Ms. Sheila was definitely going to call the police. And then from there, they would have a lot of questions to ask and a murder investigation to pursue.

He knew it wasn't a good thing any longer to have Ms. Sheila to go back to his mother's house and that he needed someone else to do so. Melvin's instincts kicked in. He texted back the number to the anonymous person to at least question why. Why would he do something like go to his mother? Or why he had done something wrong to her instead of doing it to him, if the problem was with him? He got halfway through typing the message he was intending to send then deleted it. He came to the conclusion that he wouldn't get any answers no way. Besides, he figured that if it was Mitch who sent it, he was too street smart and wise enough to know to destroy the phone.

Yvette had gone back to the bed and left Melvin to himself. He had his head hanging low. A feeling of guilt and sorrow overtook him. He now felt that if in fact his mother had been killed, that it was all his fault. That her murder was caused by his problems.

A dream came back to his memory. It was a bad one. One that occurred on the very night he spent the last hours there in prison before being released the next morning. He was standing graveside at his mother's burial when a spook appeared and chastised him for creating the atmosphere that led to his mother being brutally killed by an enemy of his. Melvin was a devastated man, both spiritually and physically. He didn't know what to do or which way to turn for help.

He didn't know if or not his mother was still alive. He'd been threatened with this. But still didn't know. Did someone kidnap her then murder her, and not want the body to be found? Or, was she killed and remained there in the house to be found? Many things raced through this man's mind. But what he truly felt in his spirit, was that she was dead; that his mother was no more. Why else would the anonymous person text and bring up any of this if it wasn't true?

The one and only person he knew he could count on to help see him through the situation was his cousin, Vick. He knew Vick would give solid advice on exactly how to go about dealing with everything. He called him up to let him know what was going on.

Vick answered, "What's up, Melvin? Everything good with you?" Vick was shocked that Melvin was giving him a call so soon.

"Vick! Cuz! This shit ain't good at all what I'm 'bout to say to you, my nigga."

"Damn, fam, what up now? What done happened now?"

"Look. The situation I was in that night when I came to you before I left later in the day."

"Yeah. What about it?"

"That shit done came back to haunt me, fam. Probably in the worst way."

"Say what?! How?"

"Cuz. I'm fucked up right now, my nigga."

"For real, cuz? How so?"

"My mama, fam. My muthafuckin' mama. I think that the nigga who was behind doing this, probably found out where she lived and got at her, since they couldn't get to me."

"You gotta be bullshittin' me, fam! And if it's true, then that pussy-ass nigga got no code that they stand on. And how the fuck them niggaz gonna involve an old lady in a beef that don't got nothing to do with her?!" Vick vented.

"I'm not saying that that's what happened. All I'm saying is, there's something going on in the area of it."

"Why you say that though?"

"Because, I been trying to call mom all last night and all this morning. She's not picking up. And I know for sure that my mama don't go anywhere at this hour of the morning. And then, I got a fuckin text message from some strange number that said something about they got her, and that everything was my fault on why she was hit and not me," Melvin acknowledged, making his cousin totally aware of it all.

"Do the nigga got her held hostage or something. Or you don't know right now?" Vick needed to know the specifics to better help.

"Nah, fam. From the sound of things, I don't think they kidnapped her or anything like that. I believe she might still be there in the house."

"So, what you specifically need me to do, cuz? You want me to go by and see what's up?"

"Yeah, cuz. That's exactly what I need you to do, to go by the house and see what's up for me. And you probably gonna have to break in. But be sure to use the back door to do so, not the front, okay, Vick. And fam...." Melvin sentence trail off. He'd began to choke on his words. Tears became heavy in his eyes. The emotion showed up.

"If my momma in there, just leave and get out. Call the police from a throwaway phone, because you know they gonna wanna know something. And most definitely gonna investigate shit about a homicide," Melvin said.

"And if that's true, what we supposed to do about getting back at the nigga who put the hit out?"

"We'll deal with that when we have to. But for right now, let's just find out the truth of the matter."

"A'ight, fam. I'm about to head over that way now. I'll hit you back later with everything."

"A'ight."

The call ended.

In between the time Melvin awaited Vick to call back and give him confirmation, he began to prepare himself for what could be really bad news. His gut feeling had him prepared to believe that his mother was a goner; that she'd been killed on the orders of Mitch as an act of retaliation for dealing with his daughter, and for siding with Mr. Raymond against him. And only if Melvin knew that the guy he shot and killed in the failed home invasion was the nephew of Mitch, then he'd know without a doubt that it was him who was responsible for slaying his poor mother.

Melvin's thoughts ran wild. He thoroughly contemplated on the best way he would be able to get the drop and hit Mitch specifically, not someone other than him.

Vick made it to Mrs. Irene house. He had a really hard time breaking into the place because of the burglar bars, but, nonetheless, he was able to. And once inside, he checked for her in the living room and in the kitchen first. No sign of her. He made a pit stop at the bathroom while en route to the bedroom. No sign of her there. And finally, he went into the bedroom where the fatality took place. There she lay, Ms. Irene, dead on the floor facing upward. She was swollen about the head, face, and body. Vick produced a look of sadness about his face and demeanor, while taking in the reality of the situation he laid eyes on.

How the fuck some nigga do this to Ms. Irene? he thought, slowly shaking his head at the same time.

As bad as he wanted to reach down, pick up her up, and wipe the gooey froth like substance from around her mouth, he couldn't. The end result of the brutal strangulation wasn't a pretty sight. Vick needed to hurry and get out of the house before someone stopped by and took notice of what was going on. He did just this. And in a rather quick manner.

On his way back to the house he had with his girlfriend, Lulu, Vick called Melvin to give him the news.

"Yeah, cuz! What's the word?" Melvin asked nervously.

"Not good, cuz! Not fuckin' good at all," Vick let out in a dreadful tone. He then paused to let Melvin have the proper time to process what he was about to say before he delivered the news.

Melvin dropped his head low and began to cry. His emotions could be heard through the phone by the cousin. Vick spoke up once more.

"I'm sorry, fam. Your mom dead. She's gone. They killed her, man. And from the looks of things, it appeared like she had been choked to death. Again, cuz, I'm sorry I had to be the one to give you this news. I truly am." He expressed his condolences for the second time.

"Yeah," Melvin replied with a deep hurt in his voice before he dropped the phone from his hand to the floor and just sat on the couch. He began to mourn for his mother uncontrollably as he lay down to rest then and there.

Yvette made her way back over to him. Melvin was now curled in the fetal position on the couch of the suite.

Not knowing what the cause for his emotion was, she took the initiative to get close to him and began to console her boyfriend to the best of her ability. She caressed him on the hand, arm, shoulder, and back, as he cried. He slightly wailed even, behind the fact of his mother being murdered. The slaying of Ms. Irene was a direct result of the ill omen that he created, the son. How was Melvin going to be able to go on with life and have the ability to deal with himself in knowing this to be true? It would continue to be a tough situation for him to find healing from for a very long time to come.

Chapter 12

SPECIAL Agent Ursula Corbin, aka "Yolanda," was again thrust back into action on the government's mission to further infiltrate and eventually take down Raymond Stephens and his long-time criminal associate turned foe Mitchell Collins. During her time away and regrouping at the training academy in Quantico, Virginia, there arose a need to review all the case notes she had, the history report, and many financial transactions that she had direct knowledge of, or was later made aware of.

Her return to Miami involved a totally different method than the position taken before. The new objective would now include Melvin in the fray, since she learned through recorded conversations that Mr. Raymond had withdrawn thousands of dollars from his bank account to pay Melvin with. And documentation and banknotes showed that the funds were to pay an important employee of his with the name named, for personal security services and other miscellaneous duties he performed.

Two investigations were tied together and could be worked through one individual: Melvin. He was the piece between them both. This was now the objective of the special task force that was aiming to nail them. For the most part, the operation was working and producing results. Although experiencing a slight twist and turn of events here and there. Nonetheless, the government still had a solid case that they were making.

A different safe house was provided for Agent Corbin on her return. It was in Boca Raton, Florida, far out of the way from the trenches in Miami when necessary to get away. But, while away, she kept in contact by phone with Mr. Raymond and Melvin. This was so to not to raise any level of suspicion as to her whereabouts or whether or not she was someone other than they knew her to be.

Yolanda's story to them about her being gone was that, she was back-and-forth between New Orleans and Atlanta, looking after family and working, doing the same thing in those two cities as she had there in Miami. She knew quite well that Mr. Raymond would always take her in and provide her with work of some sort. This was due to the business rapport that they had, and due to the crazy thought he held onto of sexually having her at least one time.

He basically would do anything to please Yolanda, as he seemed to always go above and beyond to impress her. So, to gain the special attention from someone he thought he knew, that someone who was a special agent and determined to put him away in prison, he treated her often. Sometimes when it wasn't even necessary.

Aside from the work being put in on the Raymond Stephens investigation, another federal case developed between things for Yolanda. The friend, Rachel, was missing and now presumed dead. She was the only key witness to a brutal murder by the kingpin she dated. Rachel was needed to connect the ex-boyfriend to the crimes that she reported to Yolanda. Without Rachel, there could be no corroboration to physical evidence that she left behind in those lock boxes she provided Yolanda the keys to. Her disappearance would weaken the case.

Yolanda reached out to Mr. Raymond by phone. She wanted to be made aware of what he may have going on. The numbers they had for each other was still the same.

"Ray here." Mr. Raymond answered the phone, knowing it was Yolanda that called

"Mr. Ray. Hey there. How you been?" she responded.

"I'm well, Yolanda. And yourself?"

"I've been good, Mr. Ray. I can't complain. And I hear you've been busy lately. We haven't had a chance to have a conversation in a while."

"Nope. We haven't. And yes, I've been very busy. This being a politician thing is a unique challenge for me. But if you know me, then you know that I'm up to the task. I set my sights on the mayoral office of Miami-Dade for a specific reason. Because I felt this could be a reality. I thought it was time for a Black leader to manage the city and to do an excellent job while at it," Mr. Raymond expressed.

"I'm sure that the transition has to be worth it, to draw your interest, for you to go from the private world to that of a public figure. From a profit to a set wage. What's the catch to that?"

"The catch to it, is the power that comes with being in public office. The benefits as well that come along with the position. This was what compelled the man of my stature to hop into the loop and pursue the seat of mayor."

"Well, you and I previously discussed the fact that if I wanted to get on board and move toward the future with you and that in mind, I'd always have a position, right?"

"Yes, that's what I said. And you already know that I'm a man of my word all the way. I figured that you'd return at some point soon. I really wanted you to be there when I launched my campaign bid to become mayor. But this never happened."

Portions of his campaign speech was written and touched upon for all of those who he presumed was loyal to him when the official announcement was made.

"My apologies for not making it, Mr. Ray. And you know had I not been preoccupied with serious family business, I would have been front and center," she responded.

"And there's no doubt in my mind that you wouldn't have. But this world that I now play in, it's totally different.

The responsibilities and obligations," Mr. Raymond stated with a tone of sophistication to his voice. He only spoke like this to others he knew had a level of vocabulary about themselves. Yolanda was one.

"Mr. Ray, although I danced from time to time and had seniority over other dancers, that didn't diminish the high education and learning I have. I'm thoroughly cultivated, and I hold a standard. A high standard," Yolanda stated to her ex-boss. What was implied was that, she was very much sophisticated, and had a mind that was politically correct.

"Is that right?" Mr. Raymond let out. He had to smile to himself at the witty response of Yolanda. "Now, see, that's what I'm talking about right there, Yolanda. I need somebody who's quick and nimble with words and is always eager to set things straight with the reporters, who I'm sure we gonna encounter at many times on this journey. Not to mention the fact that there's no hypocritical material attached to my name and profile. I could really use you as a spokesperson of the campaign, or as a campaign strategist. Which title would you prefer?" he asked.

"Well, I thank you, Mr. Ray, for the opportunity, as I knew without a doubt that we'd reach some type of agreement here in high society. This was the basis of everything we had with our previous business relationship. But, to answer you, I feel as though being a part of the campaign strategy team, will suit me best. My skills and knowledge are grounded in the management area anyway." Yolanda graciously accepted.

"What about the higher position as actual campaign manager itself? That's more of an executive position for you?" he offered. Mr. Raymond knew that if he was able to convince Yolanda to accept this position as campaign manager, he would essentially have her closer to him. He would be able to engage her more intimately with conversations, provide gifts, and do the whole nine while in a high pursuit to have her sexually. This was his ultimate objective. He loved women. He'd turned into a voluptuary and had no problem showing this side of himself.

"How could I refuse that, Mr. Ray?" she responded in a fond like tone of voice.

"Awesome, it's yours now. I'll simply bump the others out the way to something else and place you in that position. You're more than qualified and apt for the job than Felicia is. Are you available this coming Sunday?"

"Yes, I will be," she replied.

"Good. I'll have you meet me and a few others for dinner then. That way, I can introduce you to my personal group who's associated with the campaign. Then, on Monday, I can get you registered and all else to officially be a member on the team."

"That'll be great, Mr. Ray. I'm so excited to get to work."

"Okay, good. And what type of food you got a taste for? I'mma let you do the choosing, Miss Campaign Manager."

"Mr. Ray, you already know I'm a huge fan of Japanese food," Yolanda said to him.

"I kind figured you'd say that. It's why I took the initiative to go ahead and make reservations at Zumas on Biscayne Boulevard Way for 4:00 p.m. Is that a good time?"

"That's perfect for me."

"Well, Sunday at four it is then. And I'm sure you'll come dressed appropriately," Mr. Raymond said.

"Now, come on. You know I will. And I thank you, Mr. Ray, for keeping the door open for me and offering me this opportunity," Yolanda responded.

"By the way, where you staying nowadays?" He had personal reasons why he wanted to know this. As long as he had known Yolanda and as long as she'd been working for him at his club, he never asked her this. It was the first time.

"Where I staying nowadays?" She thought over his question. "Oh, I got a place over in the Robin Hood section of town. In fact, this where I now am," she said. This was where the previous spot was that she lived before being temporarily pulled.

"Being here in this apartment is cheap. It gives me the chance to hold on to some of that money you blessed me with when the club was sold," she mentioned. "You and Mitch sold rather." Yolanda had no idea of the heated situation that Mr. Ray and the former friend were going through.

At the utterance of Mitch's name, it triggered ill feelings and disgust in Mr. Raymond. However, he never once revealed how he thought or felt about Mitch to her. He just kept it to himself.

"Yeah, I'm sure you making good use of all that money, ain't you?" he let out with a slight chuckle.

"You damn skippy, I am," she remarked. This was a line that she'd stolen from an episode of the TV show, Martin. One of her favorites.

"Well, I gotta go for now, Yolanda. You be good, okay."

"I'll be sure to do that, Mr. Ray, and I'll see you Sunday," she said.

"I'll be sure to do that, Mr. Ray, and I'll see you Sunday," she said.

"Absolutely," he replied and concluded the call.

Yolanda had made an audio call through the Skype app once reactivating the account.

The reality of the situation was that, Yolanda previously turned over the money gave to her from Mr. Ray. Her superiors in the bureau had it. The activities of how she got it, who it came from, and for what purposes, was all documented at the completion of the recorded conversation. And the recent phone call they had, this too was documented for the purpose of evidence to be used later down the line. The case was active again. The kingpin turned politician, was placed back squarely between the crosshairs.

Chapter 13

MITCH made it priority to call a family meeting between he and the male members of his, to discuss the recent events that had effected their crew. Other than him being the one with the highest rank and respect of the eighteen that were there, he had a nephew—Vino—that hadn't long returned to the States from Haiti, and was eager to get down to business. This meant either getting money hustling, or dirtying his hands some other way like murder, or perhaps robbery again. And now, with his brother Roland being missing, Vino had a serious chip on his shoulder.

According to how Mitch chose to reveal the fact about Roland, he told them that the nephew was kidnapped in a botched home invasion, was shot, then later taken and killed. He wasn't going to be found. At no time did anyone question this. All that they knew was that the person who Mitch said was responsible, he had to get it, because of this.

Once gathered at Mitch's house, he treated refreshments, champagne, and bowls of exotic weed to smoke. He started the meeting with a few worthy remarks.

"Dear family of mine. I hereby like to call you to attention," he stated. He was draped in a cocaine white suit with pin-stripes, and had on a purple bow tie.

Everybody stopped talking, got quiet, and the meeting came to order. Mitch was standing in the center of the room and now had all eyes on him.

"Okay, so here's an update on the business of the family. But first this. The payback in blood, has been done, for Roland's death. The nigga who I found out was responsible, he couldn't be found. But, I was able to have the nigga's momma touched. And that, I did," he revealed. Everyone yelped in excitement and clapped at the news. It was like they were at a soccer game, and the team was rooting for had scored a goal.

Mitch continued. "The momma was the one who paid the price for the sins of her son." They all clapped again and expressed relief at the information. "And the moment that this bitch-ass nigga come up for air out of hiding, he's gonna get it too!" Mitch stated.

"As y'all can see, Vino back with us," he said, pointing at the street general. "He brought special gifts from our motherland for us. We'll get to that part in a minute. But the thing is this. I wanna update you all on the progress of this thing of ours," he boasted, stabbing downward with a fore-finger toward the table to gesture.

"I wanna bring to everyone's attention how we gonna go about doing business with the crews that we over." The nephews and the cousins there with him operated as captains and lieutenants.

Mitch poured himself a glass of champagne, took a sip, then continued to lecture.

"I'm sure I done made all of y'all aware of the fact that me and Ray no longer in business together. On no level! I don't have nothing to do with that sucker-ass nigga no more! He's a bitch! And I intend to deal with him when the time comes. But with the product that we were once being supplied through him, it's no more. A new connect will be supplying us from now on."

They all nodded in agreement with what Mitch said about the direction they were going to go.

"Okay, now the club thing. I was finally able to get the building renovated to how I want Club Pressure to be. We should be opening the doors soon. Everything was paid for with the money that this family produced. So, what that mean is, it's ours. The Duvalier and the Collins family. We not gonna let nothing, or no one, come between the family again. We stand for our lives, and the survival of our family depends on the protocol and principles that we putting into effect this day. We all about to go over the rules and set the record straight now, before we walk out the door. Because once we do go on about our way, nobody can't say they didn't know or wasn't told. So y'all getting it now. Consider yourselves informed and warned," advised Mitch.

His overall objective was to rewrite the unwritten book that governed the family. Mitch wanted to fix it to where none of the mishaps or misfortunes that any of them were subjected to make, would have any effect on others, as was the issue with Tisha, his own daughter, going up against him and disobeying his orders. His way of trying to retaliate caused the death of his nephew.

Mitch spoke on. "I know about the whispering that may been echoing about my daughter, Tisha. So I feel the need to get ahead of it and address that too. And finally, I can put that to the rest. Me and Tisha don't got anything to do with each other. It's been this way for a couple of months now. And to be clear, I'm talking business-wise. Not from a personal perspective. She still my daughter, and I love her. But she betrayed me. And I had to cut her off. I took care of that other issue along the way too. Nonetheless, that's something personal that has to be worked out between the two of us. And as soon as we get a hand on the nigga she's dealing with and put his ass away, the better off we'll be. So, now that we got that out of the way, let's move on to other things. Besides, I'm getting too old for this shit. I gotta leave it all to you younger folks," Mitch said. They all shared a laugh at the humor of the sixty-one-year-old Mitch.

The nephew, Hattian Vino, was seated to the right side of Mitch. He was the one next in line to succeed him and lead the family. Vino's recent trip to Port-au-Prince was to commune with family, and also, be re cloaked with divine and spiritual blessings from the ninety-year-old grandmother of his. She was the mother of his father and Mitch's mother as well. The elder lady was a highly decreed voodoo priestess. Vino saw to it as well that all of the money that the family made and sent to their homeland, was being appropriated for homes, businesses, and several other enterprises that they'd put together on the strength of the money.

The Collins and Duvaliers also thoroughly invested into rebuilding portions of the country after the devastating earthquake of 2010 that claimed the lives of some three hundred thousand people. The finances put toward the infrastructure system was the most important investment that Mitch and his family made of them all. So was the sewer system, since the males of the family at some particular point throughout their lives, were Bayakou men of the city. These were workers who held the responsibility to clean out the shit holes there. These were pit toilets that had to be cleaned by hand all throughout the city. Port-au- Prince's precarious sewer system rested on the shoulders of these men, Exilian Collins—Mitch's father, and others.

Mitch continued with all he wanted to say. "The plan from here moving forward for all of you," he pointed a finger and waved it from right to left, "is that you all report to Vino for everything, for the most part. Y'all would only see me here for meetings every first of the month, or at times, we'll meet at the club. But my duty now is to fall back and let Vino lead the way."

Mitch took a seat at that point to let Vino stand and say something to the family. The tone of his voice was a balance between husky and raspy. He spoke in a calculated manner, pointing out many things as he elaborated. He stood at six feet two and weighed approximately one hundred ninety pounds. He had a lean and athletic physique, and had a dark complexion skin tone. Dude also had a head full of dreadlocks. They were all at least ten inches or longer, and was pulled to the back into a ponytail and held together by a rubber band.

The new leader of this family sported a five o'clock shadow of a beard. He had a sharp razor lined up to the head and face. The diamond studded earrings piercing his ears sparkled heavily. They heightened the effect of his aura. Vino's appearance would put somebody in the mind of the vicious street drug kingpin Marlo Stanfield on the gripping HBO TV series, The Wire. Vino made it a priority at that point to pass out the gifts he had for everybody there. They were individually Talisman, Charms. They'd been dipped in the blood of a sacrificed animal and prayed over by the grandmother, the Voodoo Priestess. Each piece was a miniature glass design that was roughly the size of a tube of chapstick and had assorted colors to the bottles. Also, the charms were connected to a beaded necklace, much like the ones that came with dog tags. Vino had everyone to dab on a portion of the oil from the gifts. And at the same time, he read aloud a handwritten scripture the grandmother prepared. It was a prayer to be recited in their native Haitian-Creole tongue.

When the meeting ended, they went their separate ways with the importance at mind to be sure to carry out the duties that they had, and to follow protocol. The Duvalier-Collins reign, was destined to be a powerful team of people in the underworld of Miami. All that was left to do was to take a position at the docks of the Port of Miami. With the help of Nephew Vino, Mitch was able to connect with a supplier for the drugs he distributed. This was to a Dominican source with money paid in advance. The supplier had the products safely shipped from the DR to the P.O.M. From that point, it was on Mitch and his crew to pick up everything and get it to their safe house. This wasn't a problem either.

Chapter 14

MELVIN eased his way back into Miami, so he could properly bury his mother. He chose to have a private service. Invite only, was for all who were to show up and pay their last respect. There were roughly eight people he called on. Melvin feared that the police had a warrant out for his arrest for both of the shootings he committed, and for the person he killed inside the duplex. So, no chances could be taken by letting the ops get the opportunity to take him out too. Enough damage had already been done by the murder of his mother. It had to end somewhere. But not until he was to clap back and take out somebody who close to Mitch, or Mitch himself.

The people present were of course Melvin's daughter, Sherita, Ms. Sheila, Vick, Traci, three good lady friends from Ms. Irene's church, and lastly, Ms. Irene's hairdresser, Jewel. It was a brief graveside funeral. Ms. Irene's pastor officiated.

Once the coffin was lowered into the ground, Melvin and Traci made their way to her house. He really needed to get a peace of mind. Rest was necessary. However, Traci wanted to talk. She began demanding answers from him, and she left him with no choice but to let her in on all that was going on with him. He was allowed to nap first and promised he'd speak when he got up.

One the other hand, Sherita was to stay at Ms. Irene's house. She was dependent on to clean up the place the day after the funeral. And she and others were needed to get Ms. Irene's things and donate them to her church.

The idea was to let Sherita live in the house for as long as she liked, as her father had plans to be back-and-forth between Florida and New York City. He was really busy trying to process everything that had happened to him, in the fucked up way it had, ever since the day he's gotten out of prison. He was determined to put a finger on exactly where he went wrong. How did he get to the point of being shot at. People was still hot on his trail, maybe? Gunning for him. And worst of all, how did he let his personal problems find their way to the doorstep of his mother? After a three hour rest period, Melvin got up. There sat Traci on top the bed next to him, eager to talk. She took the occasion then and there.

"Melvin. Are you gonna talk about any of this before you up and go back to wherever in the world you now live?" Traci asked. She had no idea where he had been staying. There was a level of hard feelings on her behalf over all of it, because she felt as though Melvin was still her boyfriend, and that he was supposed to open up to her on these types of things. At least this was how she thought.

"What you talking about, Traci, huh? What you wanna talk about?" he responded.

"Everything, if this is possible? I wanna talk about it all. Because how do I know that my life not in danger?" She expressed to him there was a grave concern for her own well-being.

"How do you know your life not in danger?" he retorted. "Because I'm telling you, Traci, your life is not in danger. Now, how does that sound?" Melvin's words had a pitch of sarcasm to them. Traci got the hint.

"Okay, so you still refusing to tell me what the fuck going on, huh?" She got kind of loud with him. Maybe this was fear, or maybe she was tired of being not in the know.

"Everything all good, T. I'm sure it's all over with now."

Traci gave him a look as if to say. It can't possibly be over with. Somebody killed your mother all because they couldn't get to you, and more than likely, they still out there. A long pause came about through their exchange of words, then Traci spoke again.

"Melvin. Baby. Look. Look at me please." He turned his head to lock eyes with her. The downcast look was still visible on his face. He was in serious emotional pain.

"What the hell going on, Melvin, to force somebody to kill your momma because they couldn't get to you?!" she demanded to know.

She had to utilize her most calming and concerning tone of voice when speaking on this subject. She couldn't say anything that would trigger him and cause his anger to be directed at her. Tears welled in his eyes as he looked on at Traci with a blank expression.

"Melvin, it's not hard for me to put two and two together and figure this out. The night before I took you to Jacksonville to get on the train to God only knows where, you came running my way from some serious situation you were involved in. I knew something had to be really bad, since you needed me to take you all the way to Duval instead of you just going to the train station on 79th Street. And not long after, this happens to your momma. Now, how is this not that serious for me to fear for my own life? Or, it's not so serious to where you can't tell me what's going on?"

Melvin remained silent. He wanted to think carefully over his words before he was to speak again. He knew he had to give her some form of answers, because with him knowing Traci, she wasn't going to let up until she had them.

"Traci, I didn't wanna tell you what was going on because I ain't want you to panic. And I didn't wanna hurt you or your feelings no kind of way," he said to her.

"Melvin. How long me and you been dealing with each other? Wait, long enough for me to know you really good, right? Basically, what I'm saying is that, we been through deep shit together on more than one occasion. And not one time did I walk away and abandon you, did I? And not one time have I tried to get even with you behind all the fucked-up shit I know you doing on me behind my back! Not once, have I?" Traci let out. She appeared to have found her proper moment to finally vent.

"Nah, I honestly can't say you have," Melvin responded.

"So, what's stopping you from letting me know what's really going on?" Her demand to be informed wouldn't let up. She had to know. She needed to know.

"Okay, Traci. You got it. You win. I ain't got no problem with telling you what the situation is, alright? You wanna know?" Melvin said.

"No. I need to know, for my own safety. And to be able to help you."

"Alright!" Melvin shouted, raising his hands in a gesture to concede. Then, he went on to speak about the situation and what he wanted her to know.

He'd taken in the fact that she was concerned. Directly in the moment, Melvin's phone rang. It was the other girlfriend from up north calling, Yvette.

He replied with a quick text. "Can't talk now. I'll call you back later." He couldn't afford to upset Traci with any more of his drama than he'd already laid on her. He continued to explain.

"So, as I was about to say, Traci, the issue is this." He began to formulate in his mind a litany of half-truths to feed Traci. Basically, it would be a lie with sprinkles of the truth in it.

"But, before I get all the way into it and let you know, you can't get mad about any of this. And you can hold it against me either. That's all I ask. Because my momma dead behind this shit. And I'm now here with you. So let's work it out and move on," he stated, trying to urge Traci to empathize with him and the situation.

"I'm listening. Melvin. Would you please get on with telling me what the situation is? I would really appreciate it," she responded.

"Alright, I will. Here we go. So, look, I met this female at the club. Her dad was part owner of it. Anyway, throughout us dealing with one another, he had a tendency to show up at her house unannounced and at odd hours of the night. He noticed me there a few of the times but never said anything about it. Even though I did work for him and the other owner of the club. And this wasn't good for business. Turns out the reason he would show up the way he did was because, he utilized the daughter's house as a place to stash money and other shit. Long story short, a home invasion took place. The dudes who did it took her hostage. She was forced to tell them where everything was hidden at. Also, they demanded that a ransom payment be made before they was to let her go. The daddy was a major nigga in the game, and the kidnappers wanted two hundred thousand or else. Dude eventually paid the money to save his daughter. They finally let her go."

"So, they held her hostage long enough until the money was paid?" Traci asked.

"Yeah, that's what happened. So, anyway, the girl goes on to explain to the daddy that while they held her hostage, they smacked her around and whatnot. Then, they lied to her, saying that the new boyfriend of hers—meaning me—was the one who set her up to be robbed. How else would they have known what was being stashed at the house? That it clearly had to have been somebody who knew that the daddy hid things there somewhere. Or at the club perhaps. She didn't believe a word that they said because she knew better. However, the daddy, he didn't buy any of that; the story she gave to him about me. He believed that I did have something to do with it. But the female did eventually go on and tell me what the deal was with her and her dad, how he was thinking. She said that I may need to fall back for a time being from coming over to her house, and we could meet up with each other at a house one of her cousins owned in South Miami Heights. Since the daddy believed that I had something to do with the home invasion and him being out of two hundred thousand dollars, in addition to the half million in cash and dope these dudes took from the house, he wanted smoke behind it. He felt the need to do something about it," Melvin related.

"Okay. What else happened after that?"

"What you mean, what else happened after that? He told the daughter not to fuck with me no more. And he put out a hit on me to be robbed then killed. He wanted the daughter out the way by the time his goons was to track me down. But then, later found out that we were still seeing each other. We was together on the night they came to get me. This was the same night when I came running to you for you to take me to Jacksonville. A shootout took place. I know I hit one of the guys," he said as he took a pause with telling the story to see what Traci's reaction would be.

She had been busy trying to process it all. Eventually, she spoke.

"The guy you hit during the shootout, he must have died. But they didn't have to involve your momma in anything. And they for damn sure didn't have to do what they did to her. They were all the way wrong for that. But back to this female you were dealing with." Traci felt the need to specifically know about her.

"Yeah, what about her?" Melvin responded. "And no, we not still seeing each other. And I haven't had any type of dealings with her since that night."

"Okay, what's your plan moving forward? What do you intend to do?"

"Whether you agree with me or not, it ain't but one thing I can do. I gotta get back at them niggaz. The girl's daddy of all people, because they brought my muthafuckin mother into this. Pussy-ass niggaz! Done killed my mama. All of this was behind some shit I ain't even have shit to do with. So I gotta straighten my face, baby. That's all there it is to do. The one and only option. Revenge," Melvin spat.

"Well, whatever you do, just please, please be careful, will you? Because I love you, Melvin. And I missed you. I only wish you the best. If only things wouldn't have never come to this. But it is what it is. Just handle your business and be sure you get the justice we all deserve against those who were responsible for killing Ms. Irene, okay?" Traci encouraged. Her military mindset was on full display with her words to him. It was the eye for an eye mentality that was brought to the forefront. At the mention of his mother's name, Melvin shed another tear in her memory. He clenched his teeth tighter, gritting them even more. And eventually, he came with an additional remark.

"Yeah, I'mma handle my business, alright. I'mma definitely do that. And I'mma see to it that justice I want, gets done my way," Melvin declared while looking at Traci straight in the eye.

Part Two

Chapter 15

MR. Raymond made the call to all his top guys for them to meet up once again. It was him, the nephew Little Phil, and Emanuel. A clandestine conversation was necessary. It was to take place at the main funeral home owned by Emanuel, the flamingo pink building located not too far from where the Scott projects used to be. The topic Mr. Raymond wanted to discuss was related to the functioning of the operation since the nephew was put in charge. With the fact that Mr. Raymond called himself taking a bow out from the drug business, it allowed him time to focus more on the campaign for the mayor's office that was ahead of him, and the chance to pair the nephew with Emanuel. So, to continue with the enterprise and the underworld that made him rich. The moment was upon them.

"So, Emanuel. How you been, old man?" Mr. Raymond greeted.

"I been fine, Ray. I'm still here. Thank the lawd," Emanuel responded. They both shared a smile at one another.

"And yourself, nephew?" Mr. Raymond turned to greet Phil Jr.

"Uncle Raymond, I'm good to go," he replied. The meeting then got on the way.

"Okay, so, what's the progress report on the business?" Mr. Raymond jumped straight into it.

"We've sold out almost everything from the last shipment down to twenty units of the crystal stuff. And as you know, it's the biggest seller in nowadays. We down to twenty-five thousand of each pill too. Eight of each kind. And the operation's flowing smoothly. Ain't no fighting amongst the people that I got on the streets moving the product. Also, it ain't no outside pressure coming at us from the competition. Nothing from the rivals. And the police we got on payroll, they been taken care of too. It's all good. Life is good," Phil Jr. related.

"I'm glad to hear that. And I assume everything on your end is the same as well, Emanuel?" Mr. Raymond replied.

"As far as I can tell, it is," Emanuel replied.

"Okay, so the next move we need to make is to pump more money into the areas we could benefit from the most. That's in the real estate market. The popular fast-food franchises. And into the wine business that I got out in California. These the markets that's doing numbers. You been doing a good job, nephew. Keep up the good work. You too, Emanuel. Oh, and nephew, I never asked about your security. How is that?"

"We alright in that area. I'm almost always out the way from everything. This keeps me free from being vulnerable to any threat that may come about. I only show up at high stakes Poker games every now and again like you do. Or, I'll go to some other gambling spot and play skins with the boys for a few hours. That's about it. I got a select number of mean niggaz on the team that don't play around if push comes to shove," Phil Jr. mentioned.

"That's good. It's tight like you got it. The role that you filled was a tough one. But it didn't take you long to figure out how it goes and take responsibility to properly oversee the business. We got our numbers here. They low for how many people we got in the circle. But it's like this for a reason. Remember, less is more. The less people we gotta watch and concern ourselves with, the better for us," Mr. Raymond stated as he gestured with his forefinger, pointing to each one of them individually. They all smiled at one another.

Mr. Raymond then continued speaking. "This man right here, nephew," he let out, laying a hand on the shoulder of Emanuel. He stood across from Phil Jr. "Is the best friend of your father. They used to roll together every single day. They had serious history and even more serious stories that could be told about them. Legendary stories, I tell you." His words were a compliment to the legacy of the brother that was no longer with them, and to the friend who carried on the tradition with him.

"I was way younger. But I remember Emanuel back in the day, all those times he would chill with my Pop at the house to handle their business," Phil Jr said.

Mr. Raymond continued. "And now that we're in a new era, it's time for the three of us to continue to handle our business in the same way. Because I'm sure that if anything, this is what Phillip would have wanted. But at the same time, I know that the level you're on now, nephew, is a whole new world for you. A brave new world. One that you can blossom and grow in as you witness the transition I'm now making myself," Mr. Raymond stated.

"You wanna know something. Think about how nice it will be for the family to have one of our own to become the mayor of the city," Phil Jr. said.

"First Black mayor of Miami, nephew. You gotta be sure to keep that in mind. And although Miami Gardens had a Black mayor named Shirley Gibson when they incorporated from Carol City, Miami-Dade has yet to lay claim to one. I intend to be that," Mr. Raymond spoke.

"That'll be great. So, how's things going with that by the way, Unc?" the nephew asked.

"Not as easy as they try to make it out to be on TV with all the witty interviews, the thought-provoking commentary, and with all the political talking heads thinking up quick stuff to say. Nonetheless, I believe my chances to make it are pretty damn good," Mr. Raymond remarked.

"And that would be nice, Ray, to see you where you come from to be elected as the mayor and leader of this glorious city. Lord knows how nice that would be, my brother. And my strongest belief is that you'll make it," Emanuel spoke.

"I'm sure I will too, Emanuel. That's why I tossed my hat into the campaign ring. Because I got what it takes to make it, or to be the head of the city. And there ain't nothing, and I mean nothing, that's gonna stop me! I'm destined to be this. I put my soul on that," Mr. Raymond declared. They nodded in agreement and acknowledged that they was with him all the way.

Mr. Raymond continued. "As I was saying. I made it top priority to separate the two professions," he let out, then placed a hand on the shoulder of Phil Jr. "Remember Junior, I made you the first lieutenant to oversee the operations that brings in the money. And I done opened the door for us in the political world. And ol' Emanuel, here," he worded. He turned to look at him and placed a firm grip on the shoulder of the elder. He's the swing man and the financial counselor to our family. You been this way for quite some time now. We all shall continue to make progress like we are. And might I have you to know, I'm in the process of welcoming back into our circle a few others," Mr. Raymond stated to make them aware.

Emanuel and Phillip Jr. both appeared to be taken aback by the words that came out of Mr. Raymond's mouth.

"Who might that be, Unc?"

"Calm down, nephew." Mr. Raymond detected concern in his voice. "No need to worry. You already know I'm too smart to be stupid. I would never have brought anyone to you we don't know or somebody we can't trust. It's my girl, Yolanda," he revealed.

"Oh, you talking 'bout that fine honey complexioned female who used to work at the club, right?" asked Phil Jr.

Emanuel produced a subtle frown about his face behind the mentioning of this woman. He knew exactly who Mr. Raymond referred to, and he hated the thought.

"Why you holding a look like that, Emanuel?"

"I got too much to say on that. You already know how I feel about that girl you got working with you. So I'mma just keep quiet and let you lead," stated Emanuel. "if it's the same one you had to come by to pick up money before?"

"To answer your questions, nephew, yes, she's the one," Mr. Raymond stated to provide clarity. "She's back. And more than likely, I'mma have her putting in more work and running more errands for me in the near future."

"If she on the team, it means she's off limits to everybody, huh?" his nephew asked.

"That's exactly what that means, nephew."

"Okay. So on to another question."

"I'm listening."

"What about the other dudes who used to work for you at the club? The ones who so happened to have a foot in the game too. I'm talkin' 'bout Big Mix, Bo Jack, and the other one?" Phil Jr. asked.

Emanuel dropped his head at the utterance of Big Mix's name. He knew what the reality of the situation was with Big Mix, that he was no more.

"Jerome not around no more, nephew. And Bo Jack and the others, chose to take sides with Mitch when we had our little fallout," Mr. Raymond responded.

"How you feel about that entire situation anyway? You think Mitch may end up being a bigger problem than we originally thought?" Phil Jr. asked.

"No, I don't think so. It wouldn't be good for business for him. Besides, I've transitioned into the world of being a public figure now. It's gonna hurt his pride and ego more than anything to see my face and my name on all the campaign posters and signs. He knows what'll happen if he was to come for me. He knows he won't have no success in that type of way. So I had come to figure that he'll try to do something else to steal my shine and have the limelight on himself for a change. You know he's so-called himself done opened up that little piece of shit for a nightclub called Club Pressure, don't you?" related Mr. Raymond.

They all had a loud laugh together at the mention of Mitch's new business venture. The very thought of such a low-quality club in comparison, it was a total joke to them. Mitch's new joint had nothing on K.O.D. Period.

Phil Jr. had something of interest to say.

"But to be real about it, a few of my guys I roll with say that the place is kind of live. That they like it in a way," he said.

"Garbage cans get a steak every now and then. But speaking of your guys, what's the overall status for your crew? Is everything good and quiet?" Mr. Raymond asked. "They can party. But we don't need too much partying going on."

"Oh, yeah, we all good on the streets and in the clubs. Big shit poppin' and little shit stoppin' on our end. The stash spots safe. Our turf protected. The money is always calculated and accounted for. And all of us get along good. Ain't no hating on each other. And we all making the product disappear accordingly. So, yeah, we good," Phil explained.

"You got any room anywhere for one or two more guys? I was looking to bring in a couple from the club. A few you might not know too much about. They the ones I was personally grooming and who weren't personally swayed to Mitch's side when we parted ways."

"If that's what you need me to do, Uncle Ray, I'll do it. I can slide whoever into the rotation at any time."

"Okay, good. Please do that, because these two guys I'm speaking on, are two really loyal and dedicated dudes. And one of them I'mma leave with you on a full-time basis. But for the other one, my plan is to keep him clean and eventually have him close by my side. He's from a dying breed. Really loyal and obedient to the core. He not too long got out of prison, and then came my way for a job when we were in need of someone at the time. Yolanda was told to find a man to fill the spot as a bouncer. She found him. He's a guy by the name Melvin. But in the streets, he said everybody called him by the name Parlay," said Mr. Raymond, to make the other two aware of the dude he silently looked at like they were his sons. Mr. Raymond's intentions were clearly on display. "He's a strong addition. The man did almost twenty years in prison, and I accepted him. He'll never forget that. He thanks me all the time," Raymond spoke.

"He did almost twenty years in prison, Ray?!" Emanuel asked.

"Yeah, from what I know. He told me about this first, then I researched him. Everything he said checked out," Mr. Raymond confirmed. "The boy is kind of suave too. Gotta playa bone in his body. And he's smart about how he moves. These are two main things I like about them." Mr. Raymond then adjusted his vest and a silk button down shirt he had on.

He had a thought. It was made known to the others. "Boy kind of reminds me of myself when I was his age. He looks and speak like he may be a man of leisure too. He's a smart guy. A really smart guy. And he had something going on with Mitch's daughter too. Tisha. So, at some point in the future, I may be able to use that to my advantage, if it comes to that. You remember Tisha, don't you, Phil? She was the supervisor over the bar area when we had the club going."

"Yeah, I remember her. We used to exchanged a few words, whenever I would visit the club and chill at the bar."

"But Tisha's the boy Melvin's girl, huh?"

"One of them, at least. He brought it to my attention. But look, my intention is to bring him on board and make good use of him and the skills he got. Me and him done already discussed this."

"That's what's up. I can't wait to meet him," Emanuel stated.

The subject switched up at that point.

"So, all the money checking out like it's supposed to, you say Emanuel?" Mr. Raymond asked about his financial status and the situation. It was very important to him.

"Yes, Ray. I got everything under control like I always have when it comes to the money. Me and your nephew there work well together, just the same way as me and his daddy did," Emanuel made mention of.

"Okay, good. Because Ray Jr. will be home soon to visit. I'mma need for him to take care of things on his end like he always has done. There's a plan to give him more money moving forward, to make an additional investment in New York City into the properties and developments for me, and out in California with the winery we own in Napa Valley. These are wise investments, I think. And I'm also looking into finding ways to have money working for us in Silicon Valley. So, Phil, I'mma need you to keep in contact with your cousin more often. He's gonna keep you informed on many things from a financial point of view. And also, you two will know Ray Jr. is the one that's keeping us legit. He cleaning up the money. He's moving it well. The boy smart," Mr. Raymond said of his one and only son, the Dartmouth alum.

Mr. Raymond relied upon his gay son to properly invest the money for him, particularly in one of the world's wealthiest city, New York City. The son successfully started up businesses, advanced them, and then, generated a hefty profit from them. These investment ventures became lucrative on both coasts, and it was the illicit profits from narcotics and the profit that K.O.D. brought in that made it possible. And this was a really good thing, since Mr. Raymond was looking to totally remove himself from all activities of the underworld.

It was necessary that he not put himself at risk anymore of being named in a federal indictment. This simply could not be a thing. And although he came from an illegal background and built on the one he passed on to his nephew to run, in his mind, he was no criminal. Not by far.

Mr. Raymond saw himself as somebody out of the many that had a brain and also had the mental wherewithal to use it. He really wanted to treat politics like the drug game. That's to provide the people with what they enjoyed doing. As below in the underworld, so above in the legit one. Simply put, people loved results. And he felt he could deliver.

This was one of the main reasons why he turned over everything to Phil Jr. and Emanuel, his two most trusted people. The formula for their success was rooted in the connection that there was there to the supplier. The way that the product was shipped to them. The secrecy to how they stashed all of the product they had, and in the way that the money was being invested, was there success. No one other than those three knew how their crew functioned. This was their advantage, and they had no plans to stop anytime soon. Mr. Raymond brought the meeting to an end.

His guests eventually left went their separate ways to handle their own businesses for the day. None of the three had any idea of the danger that had already found its way into what was supposed to be a tight knit circle.

Chapter 16

WITH Phil Jr. now at the head position of the crew, he was able to do a thorough job with the way he put things together. The ground work was critical. The overall scheme of everything was really important. He had a total of twenty soldiers that moved the product he supplied. Also, he had someone he knew pretty well be his personal bodyguard and driver. This was a guy by the name Emmett Lamar, but he was better known on the streets by the moniker, "Hitman."

His reputation far preceded in person. And the title alone, sent fear throughout the streets. Hitman was somebody that gained his stripes and due respect in the hood of the Liberty City housing projects called "The Pork and Bean." He was older than the guy he worked for, but was sure to pay Phil Jr. the same level of respect that he did the father when he was around. Hitman was a teenager when Big Phil reigned on 15th Avenue Northwest. He ruled with an iron fist. But had mercy and showed love. Big Phil owned the car detail shop on 79th Street and on 7th Avenue NW. Hitman worked for him there too. He also made runs and did other small errands for Big Phil and performed other chores.

One day in 1991, Big Phil called upon Hitman to take care of something of a more serious nature for him. There was a certain guy who had violated Big Phil in a major way, and for this, the head honcho wanted him whacked. The dude marked for death had managed to build up the nerve to break into the home of one of Big Phil's ladies. She was beaten badly, slashed in the face with a razor, robbed of expensive jewelry, clothing, cash, and other valuables materials, and left for dead. She survived the brutal home invasion but barely.

The perp was a dude in his early twenties by the name of Chris, better known as Rude Boy. Little Emmett knew dude from around the way, and also knew it wouldn't be too hard to catch up with him.

Chris was able to catch the girlfriend down bad to pull off the caper. He followed her home from the detail shop one day. He knew that the female had dealings with Big Phil and automatically assumed that she had to be holding heavy for him, opposite of all he saw on her. She was always draped in jewelry daily. But once completing the caper and getting off with nearly $200,000 in cash and all else, he made attempts to try and sell the custom-made pieces of jewelry to pawn shops and a few jewelers. Basically to the highest bidder. Chris had no knowledge that the thick locket charm that accompanied the herringbone necklace, had an engraving on it of a birth date and the phone number inside the gut of it.

The owner of the pawn shop who was most interested to buy it said Chris repeatedly tried to sell it, but he refused to to buy the pieces at such high price he wanted. Also, once he took notice of the engraving, this made him back out and forced him to alert would-be dealers, that something wasn't right with the material Chris was trying to sell. Additionally, the jeweler wrote down everything, so to contact the rightful owner. Later on, the call was made. It wasn't even an hour later.

But, while recovering from the attack, the girlfriend got in touch with Big Phil. She'd been released from the hospital. She told him about everything the jeweler related when he'd called. Big Phil made it top priority to stop by the particular shop to hear for himself.

Phil was shown video footage of the guy that was eager to sell. He knew then and there it was none other than Chris.

Big Phil had more patience than the average man. He didn't jump to act so fast against Chris. He sat back, waited, and paid close attention to him, to know whether it was him or not. He also wanted to know if there were any co conspirators that played tag along with Chris. There wasn't any. Now feeling the heat while in a paranoid state of mind and fear of what could come about, Chris went into hiding, and never came back around. This was additional proof for Big Phil that he was guilty of something. Big Phil got with Emmett about doing a hit, and he agreed, to the payment of $5,000.

Payment was made in advance, then, the details of who was to die came later. Emmett, at no time in his young eighteen-year-old life, had ever held that type of money. He figured if he was to do a good job, that Big Phil would call on him again for the same kind of work. This was the development stages of who Big Phil had helped create become Hitman as he was now known.

Finally, Emmett caught up with Chris. He put him away with five shots; three to the head and two to the body. He popped his "cherry," as hitters would say in committing their first murder for hire in the murder gang. Hitman eventually went on to do more, and he went all the way out in the process, taking on many contracts and performing many hits, thus bearing the name Hitman.

Over a two year period of time, a solid bond between Hitman and Big Phil developed. Whenever the need arose, Big Phil would call on Hitman, and the Grim Reaper he became, would show to pay somebody a visit. He delivered every time.

Hitman been knew Phil Jr and had been around him from time to time. He knew the uncle as well, Mr. Raymond, and in a way, Hitman was someone who was close to the Stephens family. As time passed and Phil Jr. grew older, he had a tendency to lean on Hitman for advice more on his journey through the underworld. Lately, a ruthless threat by a rival street team began to penetrate the territory where Phil Jr and the crew mostly operated.

This was the 'Opalocka' section of town, in a territory called the Triangle also the Bab. Hitman would soon be thrust into more action. He was needed o put down the boss of the crew that came with problems. Phil Jr's philosophy was to simply kill the head, and the body would follow. This logic had always stood the test of time.

Chapter 17

MELVIN reached out to Mr. Raymond. He wanted to know if it was possible that they could meet? There was a few things important that needed to be discussed. Mr. Raymond agreed to this. He already had an interest in bringing Melvin closer to him on the team and making really good use of the guy. He'd taken a liking to him. The main thing Melvin wanted with Mr. Raymond, was to be fronted a sum of money again, because his was low, and there was a waiting process he had to go through about the insurance policy payment behind his mother's death and at the bank where he was looking to inherit everything of value that his mother left behind. Another meeting between the two was already in the works before to the day. But Melvin needed to go home first.

In addition to Melvin being strapped for cash, he needed Mr. Raymond to contact the people he had on payroll that worked in law enforcement at the police department. He needed specific information. Was he or was he not, a wanted man?! Although Melvin could have tapped his cousin and asked him to do the same thing, his mind pushed him more toward Mr. Raymond since he had far more significant concern, connections, and friends in high places, than Vick did. Also, Vick was doing business in a risky game with trafficking, and needed to keep clear of contact with any police authorities. Melvin borrowed Traci's car for the day while she was at work doing a twelve-hour shift. Nobody would have had any idea that it was him in her car had they been looking for him.

Tisha knew the Tahoe truck, and he was looking to avoid her for a little more time for all of his reasons. He needed to know for certain that she had nothing to do with letting her daddy where his mother lived, because for all of those that he suspected had a hand in the murder of his mother, they were shortlisted to be executed. He was simply lining his ducks in a row, and in all actuality, Tisha was the centerpiece to it all. At least for right now.

Mr. Raymond told Melvin to meet him at his home in Palm Beach again, the one that he shared with Camille. It was located on Sea Spray Avenue. The six bedroom, four baths, two thousand one hundred and forty-four square foot, $2.5 million home rested, and for Camille to be the side piece, she really had it going on. Her treacherous, conniving ways placed her in a good situation. But as the saying goes, karma is a bitch, and the daughter of her's was no good either!

Melvin arrived at the entrance to the gated community. He was allowed access. Once reaching the front door of the home, he rang the doorbell. A slim, Hispanic female housekeeper approached and opened for him. She welcomed him inside. This was the first time the two had laid eyes upon each other. They exchanged greetings, and she escorted him to the bar area where Mr. Raymond and Camille were situated and enjoying the company of each other. They both smiled at Melvin.

The surround sound system played music by Megan Thee Stallion. Camille loved her music. She made it a priority to ensure that Mr. Raymond learned the importance of keeping with the times. This was especially true when it came to music.

"There he is!" Mr. Raymond let out. "My guy Melvin!" He got up to his feet as Melvin walked up to him and shook his hand.

"What's good, Mr. Ray! Long time since I last had a chance to see you in person. And man, am I glad to see you!" Melvin responded. He placed emphasis on his tone. The signs of being overwhelmed and distressed were on full display.

"You are. Well, we're here face to face again, my brother. And as you may know, this here is Camille."

Melvin shook her hand as well.

While they greeted one another, he turned back once more to place his focus on Mr. Raymond. His demeanor troubled the new jack political figure.

"Well, what you wanna drink? You give the appearance like you could use one. I see it written all over your face," Mr. Raymond stated.

"You right about that. And damn, that's a tough one there," Melvin let out.

Then, he moved his eyes up and down the counter, looking at the fully stocked shelves of the bar.

"I don't want anything too strong, because I gotta drive back down the highway home. But if anything, I'll sip on a little champagne," he requested.

Camille served as a bartender for this occasion. She eased behind the counter to pour up Melvin a glass of what he asked for. He pointed to the bottle of Krug. She and Mr. Raymond were enjoying the Moet. Each and every time Melvin found himself in the company of Mr. Raymond, the elder always made the younger one feel worthy and important. Melvin was handed one of the expensive cigars by Mr. Raymond. He puffed on one himself. The three of them took seats in the lounge section of the customized man cave. The design was for maximum comfort and pleasure.

"I wanna thank you yet again, Mr. Ray, for having me over and offering your time to discuss a few things with me," Melvin said to begin with what he wanted to talk about.

"My pleasure, Melvin. Our conversations in the past was those that pointed to the coming of days. Like this. Have we arrived at a point where you really need my help? What's the problem? Maybe some of this good grace and chemistry me and Camille got, can be applied to you and Tisha. Because you seem like you stressed out about something. She's the reason maybe. And you welcome to any play of mine at any time. So long as you one of the people who I got close to me," Mr. Raymond responded for all of those reasons.

It was times like these that Mr. Raymond appeared to be the most happiest, anytime he was with Camille. At least in that moment. She was the only woman that he'd ever seen him with.

Tisha had long told him the story of how Camille began cheating on her father as the two continuously had relationship problems. It was never fully discovered exactly who it was that Camille ended up being with or even where she had relocated to. All that was known was that she and Mitch were no more.

Every form of communication between the two was eventually cut off. And the fact of the matter was that, Camille, knew more about Mr. Raymond and his underworld enterprise, than the wife of his did, Christine. This had a lot to do with the business relationship and friendship that Mr. Raymond and Mitch had before it was a them. Mitch exposed her to far more than he should have, and she had a hand in the illegal activities of his and all else, rather that was transporting millions in narcotics for Mitch in the early part of their relationship, laundering money, or facilitating in a business deal by keeping the girlfriend of the buyer of his supply in good company.

The bottom line was that, she knew a lot about both men. Also, Mr. Raymond found himself taking a liking to her. This happened really early. He thought it was best to take her away from Mitch, and he made her one of his women, the first opportunity. Mr. Raymond was able to plug two holes with this one move. He had to prevent the ship he was the captain of from sinking. The first was that, he had to prevent her from exposing he and Mitch's business to some other dude she were to meet, if she and Mitch were to ever break up. He knew about the problems they had in their love life. Or worse, expose things to the police. And the second was that, he didn't have to worry any longer of Mitch potentially killing her and going off to prison.

This would have essentially sent the drug operation into total chaos, because it was Mitch and his people, that sold ninety percent of the product. And based on their work in the streets, that was how Mitch and Mr. Raymond got rich. Therefore, based on Camille knowing all that she did about both of them and because she was also an important person in their lives, Mr. Raymond took her on and kept her happy. This was how and why they came to be.

Melvin wanted to be updated on Mr. Raymond's political affairs.

"So, Mr. Ray, your campaign bid to become mayor of Miami, how's that been working out for you?" he asked.

Melvin had read and studied the book, The 48 Laws of Power, and had first-hand knowledge of how to get a man to reveal more of himself and on what he was intending to do. One of the quotes he remembered most, was that, if you talked to a man about himself, he would never stop talking. Melvin knew the sure reality of these words about Black men specifically. There was a strong tendency for them to brag about many things verbally. Especially if it was pertaining to them in some personal type of way.

"Oh!" Mr. Raymond jumped at the opportunity to offer a response. "Oh, everything is coming along well, I tell you. It's coming along very well. But you know that the actual election isn't until a year or so into the future. I felt the need to toss my hat into the race as early as possible. That way, I could establish a grassroots base of voters, and learn as I move along, all there is to know, on my way to the throne," Mr. Raymond stated with a bright smile. He took another sip of champagne from his glass and puffed on a Cubana cigar.

He twirled it in rotation between his fingers. It was as if the cigar was a miniature log on a body of water.

"I've been shown a vision, Melvin. It's my destiny to become the mayor of this magnificent city," he declared.

"It absolutely is," Camille chimed in to say, gently stroking Mr. Raymond along the cheekbone with the back of her hand, then kissed him tenderly. She appeared to be in love with Mr. Raymond.

"Politics just may be your calling, Mr. Ray. Success seems to be a part of your DNA," Melvin said to compliment. "It's there with you, all you set out to do."

"Just maybe and I know the road ahead is gonna be tough along the way, being that the incumbent mayor, who happens to be the son of the former mayor, has held onto the seat for as long as he has. Nonetheless, I strongly have faith that I shall make it through the primary stages and take him on head up."

"You got the willpower and the proper amount of determination necessary to achieve this goal. And although I had begun to love the club and had wrapped my mind around the idea of getting deeper into the profession of matters and security, being close to you and doing personal detail is something I could appreciate too," said Melvin.

"The entire reason why you here, Melvin, is because of the type of person I had come to know you to be. You're loyal. You're committed. And you're a dedicated dude. That's enough to make you worthy of being on my team. But only one thing. . ." Mr. Raymond's words trailed off and created an element of suspense. Also, he stopped short on what he wanted to say, so to let Camille have the opportunity to excuse herself from their presence. Certain things he didn't want her to know. The intended objective was to utilize Melvin as a go between with him and other people. He would also play a smaller role in line with Willie as personal security.

Melvin was a convicted felon and an ex-con. Therefore, Mr. Raymond knew that he couldn't have him associated anywhere near the official campaign. But felt comfortable in having the guy close to him on a personal level, due to the strength, promise, and potential that Melvin had. He was very determined to be somebody, and his serious desire to make positive contributions, was now a part of who he was as a reformed man. But was he really? Melvin had always wanted to be accepted by somebody in their organization. And in return, heap praise upon them. Mr. Raymond took notice of this. Why not it be me? He had come to figure that he developed a love for being revered. Mr. Raymond thought highly of himself in this regard.

"Now my interest is in you as a personal bodyguard. Also, you'll do some driving for me on an occasion too," Mr. Raymond stated.

Chapter 18

AS Mr. Raymond looked on at his guest square in the eyes, Melvin took in all that was said to him. He produced a slight smirk on his face and took adoration behind the compliment made by the former kingpin, successful nightclub mogul, and political candidate.

Finally, Melvin spoke up. "I would love to have the position to protect you and do the driving for you, Mr. Raymond." He happily accepted the offer.

It was very thing that Big Mix was doing for Mr. Raymond, outside of the club and the drug dealing. Melvin would be essentially replacing him in those positions, and of course, these particular duties, would go hand in hand with somebody that would work closely for Mr. Raymond. The job had the potential to be beneficial reward the man that filled the spot. This was now Melvin.

Mr. Raymond was really paid. He had a gang of businesses that brought in money all around the world for the people who worked for him. And these same workers had the opportunity to invest in what he owned. Mr. Raymond was a big stepper, and he was almost always looking to broaden his horizons.

He continued with what he was saying. "So, I take it that that's a yes, Melvin?" He wanted confirmation.

"Of course that's a yes, Mr. Ray. How could I say no to you? I practically owe you so much, because of the opportunity you gave me when I first got out. I had the time of my life while working at K.O.D. I loved it!" Melvin responded with a smile. He extended his hand to shake Mr. Raymond's to seal the agreement.

"Okay, now that we got that part out of the way, I wanna have a discussion with you from a real nigga perspective. And I'm sure I don't even have to ask you, because more than likely, that girlfriend of yours, Tisha, done already mentioned so much to you about the history of me and her daddy, hasn't she?" Mr. Raymond asked. His aim was eventually to know how much Melvin knew about him, other than when he's told him personally.

"Truth be told, Mr. Ray, she did. Tisha mentioned a whole lot to me about the history of you and Mitch. But me and Tisha not together like that no more. We called it quits," Melvin responded.

Mr. Raymond didn't know about any of the issues that Melvin had gone through with Mitch over his daughter. There weren't any plans in the pipeline to know, unless specifically asked. Melvin didn't want to cause any trust issues between him and Mr. Raymond. And he for damn sure, didn't want the man to begin questioning himself, as to whether not he made the right decision to bring Melvin back into the fold in working for him. So to keep things on the up and up, he knew it was best to nip things in the bud and make it known that Tisha, was old news to him.

Melvin elaborated a tad more about the dealings of him and Tisha. "I cut her loose before going up north to live. This was why I was away. I still talk to her every now and then. But even with that, we ain't done in a while. Other than that, it's a wrap on what we had. She got too much going on with her and her ways. And that nigga, Mitch . . . he don't seem to make it any better."

"You spoke the truth then with that about Mitch. But anyway, I know how Tisha has the tendency to speak on things. I'm comfortable knowing that with certain things I don't have to speak so much on, because there's always others to do it for me," Mr. Raymond said, hinting at the reputation he'd gained in the streets.

A slight pause came about between the two of them. Then, switching the subject to something much more akin to Melvin's taste, he asked the question, "You ever heard of the name Chief Phillip before?"

"You talking about the big time kingpin guy, Chief Phil, who was one of the heavyweights that ran 15th Avenue back in the day?" Melvin responded.

"Yeah! That's Chief Phil."

"Hell yeah! Who from Miami that ain't heard of him? That nigga right there, was the muthafuckin man! Mr. Ray, when I was a Jit, I did have a chance to see him a time or two. But that's about it," Melvin replied.

"Well, he was one of my brothers."

Melvin jarred his head. He was taken by surprise. He had a hard look into the eyes of Mr. Raymond. There was a degree of appreciation on Melvin's behalf in regard to Raymond and him relating whatever story he was in the process of speaking on. "Oh, he was?! Interesting. And now that you mention it, from memory, you two do look alike in a lot of ways. That dude, like you, really had it going on. It's all kind of legendary stories to this day still floating around town about him. I don't know if you know or not, but there's a lot of people who don't believe that your brother is dead. Everybody saying he faked his own death, because he was in something deep, and he couldn't get out of it. Like way In Too Deep! Similar to some shit like Freeway Rick Ross and some CIA type shit," Melvin said.

Mr. Raymond didn't respond; he simply continued to look at him and maintained his smile. *If that was the case, I'd be the first to know about my brother not being dead, but in fact still alive,* he thought.

The truth of the matter was that, there was a lot of validity to the story about Big Phil Stephens, the brother of Mr. Raymond, having faked his own death and indeed was still alive. The federal government that was after him, believed that he had escaped the country like a prisoner from incarceration and fled to some Spanish speaking nation, being that the girlfriend who was in his life at the time the supposed death took place, was fluent with the Spanish language herself, and knew too much about the business and the drug trade that Big Phil had going on.

If Big Phil hadn't faked his death, why had he up and checked himself out of the hospital after denying proper medical treatment behind a bad car accident, and there wasn't any immediate threat to his life or freedom? Why was this so? And after all, he did have a close friend and business partner in Emanuel, that owned a funeral home, one that Big Phil paid for, and could have easily had Emanuel place a similar body in his place, one that resembled his to help facilitate the escape. The bottom line was that, for whatever reasons there were for Big Phil to get gone, there ended up being no more evidence to suggest that he faked his death than there was evidence to support that he'd actually died. There was never the conclusive confirmation to any of the two.

Mr. Raymond continued with speaking again. "But yeah, Melvin, I owe a great deal of appreciation to my brother for the successes that I have experienced, the club in particular. And a few other business ventures. These were all his visions that I brought to life for him, since he wasn't around long enough to do so himself. But as for the political aspirations that I'm now living out, these are the dreams of our father," he said to Melvin.

Melvin smiled at the words of Mr. Raymond. There was a fond memory of something that passed through his mind. "Do you mean that like dreams from your father, the book Obama wrote?" he asked, still smiling.

"Yeah, like those dreams of my father, similar to the book Obama had written. You see how sharp you are. Always on point? Who would have ever thought of that other than you?"

"Yeah. Prison has its ways of how it preps you and grooms you to be on point like this," Melvin responded, his smile still on display. "After all, prison is nothing but concrete and steel, the two main tools necessary to sharpen other harden objects. Inmates can be hardened. Their hearts as well." He exhibited a deep degree of wisdom with his witty remarks.

Mr. Raymond smiled more now, having deeper degrees of satisfaction behind the decision to bring Melvin closer. "Is that right?"

"Yes, Sir! Absolutely right. And I understand you very well, Mr. Ray. I totally do. Let's move on to another subject now. How about you ain't never told me if or not you got any kids?" Melvin asked a simple question now. One he hadn't before.

"Yeah, I do. I got two daughters and a son," Mr. Raymond informed.

From the look on his face at the mention of a son, Melvin immediately took note that there must had been something about the son that Mr. Raymond highly disliked or despised even. Like the man spoke on having two daughters first, before speaking about a son. Usually, a man would take great honor and pride to speak on their sons, and would always place the mention of a son well ahead of mentioning his daughters. Not so for Mr. Raymond. Even with the fact of Raymond Jr. being the first born and bearing his name.

From how Melvin took this was that, there simply had to be something going on there, something from a serious nature.

They remained quiet. He gave Mr. Raymond a certain look. the kind of look that said, I don't understand. Please explain to me. Mr. Raymond noticed game and was brought back to reality on what Melvin's IQ level was. He was aware that the man had a great understanding of human nature. Therefore, without holding back, Mr. Raymond took the first opportunity to bring a reality to Melvin's attention.

"Yeah, see, you're pretty intelligent, Melvin," he said.

"Huh?" Melvin fake, not being able to read between the lines.

"Well, my son's not right. He's gay."

I knew it had to be something, Melvin thought to himself. "Hey, I'm not the one to judge nobody, Mr. Raymond. That's not my position. It ain't who I am," he responded.

"Yeah, I know. You a straight up type of dude, Melvin. But it was important that I let you know that, since you asked about my kids. He's wrong though. And I got an early twenties daughter and a teenage daughter. She's fifteen."

"Oh, okay. I thank you for letting me know. And for the sake of you knowing, at no time had Tisha said anything to me about your kids. I never knew anything. That's why I asked." Melvin knew the importance of putting that out there to Mr. Raymond. He didn't want the man to feel any type of way about him, like maybe he and Tisha had spoken badly about him and his son behind his back. The connection between Mr. Raymond and Melvin was far more dear to him than the eyes could see. What Mr. Raymond saw in Melvin, was the son figure he always wanted. The one he had always wished for. And likewise, what Melvin saw in Mr. Raymond, was the father figure he'd always wanted, the one he'd always wished for. The love and feelings were mutual with both of them. They greatly admired each other.

The two men continued to sip on their drinks and puff on expensive cigars as they carried on meaningful conversations.

"But real talk. You wanna know something, Melvin?"

"Yeah, what's that, Mr. Ray?"

"Tisha," he let out and wagged his index finger at Melvin while in preparation to say what it was he was intent on saying. "That was a decent catch for you there, my friend. It really was," complimented Mr. Raymond. "That chocolate baby doll that she is, is a handful, ain't she?"

"No, she wasn't. Tisha's a very good woman. It's her muthafuckin' daddy, who's the handful! He's the one who acts like a bitch all the time! Nigga was always trying to be up in her business and always got something to say. He stayed putting his nose in her relationships. Dude was too damn much for me to be dealing with, in addition to my own problems. He was one of the main reasons why I had to fall back from dealing with his daughter. But I can't say that Yolanda didn't warn me ahead of time of how overprotective Mitch was about his girls. Tisha specifically. But I was thinking that was because of the incident that happened at the club when dude knocked out her teeth. Turned out that that was far from it," Melvin stated.

"I see you been told about that too, huh? And for me, that was one of my main reasons why I had to put distance between Mitch and me. It ain't no telling what Mitch and his boys ended up doing to the guy who hit Tisha. The incident initiated inside the club. My club. Which means, if he was killed, and the police do find out about it, the investigation is gonna start with me for murder. It is the only crime that don't have a statute of limitations. The very last thing I need to be concerning myself with, is a goddamn murder rap that I'll have to go to war up against! Hell no! Not at my age! Not this late in life. And especially not so, after I've already made my exit out of the game," Mr. Raymond said with emphatically.

"Tell me about it," Melvin said to concur with his boss. The image flashed through his mind on how he popped the dude in the duplex that night, bringing an end to his life forever. Also, the reality of Big Dre began to haunt him psychologically. Melvin knew without a doubt that there was no such thing as a perfect crime. And the crime of murder, would almost always weigh heavily on the person who committed it, whether spiritually, psychologically, legally, or otherwise.

"Me and Mitch been through a lot of things together, and have done even more shit together," Mr. Raymond said, almost in a somber tone of voice. "But like I said, a goddamn murder charge, or any charge for that matter, is one that I absolutely don't wanna be ducking from. Mitch can have that!"

Melvin couldn't help but let out a chuckle behind the animated way Mr. Raymond expressed himself.

"I know that's right, Mr. Raymond." he commented then raised his glass to offer a toast.

"And speaking of our girl, Yolanda." Mr. Raymond switched gears. "She finally returned to Florida from visiting her family in other states."

"Oh, she did?"

"Yep! And you should already know better than anybody, that I like to keep her around. She was the one who found you, remember?"

"I do."

"And Yolanda is simply too valuable as an assistant for me not to keep her around. I got a spot for her on my mayoral campaign team. She's gonna be one of the main people. Her business practice is really appreciated. And although she knows a lot about me and the people who I got around me working, Yolanda don't talk about nobody. More than likely, next week, I'mma call a meeting between all of us to have dinner, so we can go over how I can move forward with the business. We're now into it heavy. And everything about the campaign will also be included. I'll be discussing the other business ventures I need assistance with as well. I'm into real estate and many other financial enterprises that I capitalize on. I own thirty companies, Melvin. I'm doing good for myself and my family," Mr. Raymond related, always being sure to praise himself.

"You definitely are, Mr. Ray. I'm always glad to say that I work for you exclusively, sir." Melvin seemed to know a thing or two about buttering up the words he was utilizing to give praise to the man of the hour.

Their casual conversation continued on for the better part of another hour, as Mr. Raymond proceeded further with his new protege. This speech to Melvin slowly revealed more of himself personally, and they added to the discussion past matters from hindsight. Mostly about things that happened at K.O.D. and those that placed Mitch into the fray.

If anybody, Mitch was a particular subject that the both of them could honestly agree on as being a low life piece of shit that he was. He had too many complexities about himself. Those that stagnated him from growing and maturing as a man, and those that hindered him. He was a problem. Mr. Raymond's separating himself from him worked out well. And from Melvin's perspective, it was an eye for an eye and a tooth for a tooth battle between them, he and Mitch. Melvin killed Roland, the nephew of Mitch, and in return, Mitch had killed Melvin's mother. For his past bad actions, this could potentially be a never ending cycle of bloodshed between the two.

Chapter 19

TISHA had gained the ability necessary to maintain herself mentally and emotionally from a nervous breakdown she had. This was after all that had happened with her and Melvin and the situation of the shootout that took place. She was still pissed to the moon and back, over how Melvin had abandoned her without so much as telling her anything. And now that she was several months pregnant with the seed that belonged to him, it was necessary she contacted him some type of way.

The depression and desperation that plagued her monthly, was from how she felt she'd been left to do it all over again by herself, and raise another child with the two she had. The problem between her and her father was still there, and he seemed to be content with having nothing to say or to do with her no more. But maybe if she was to apologize to him and make sincere amends, then and only then, might he take into strong consideration to finally let bygones just be bygones.

Nevertheless, throughout the highs and the lows, Tisha continued to maintain with her money, the cash that was brought in from the businesses she owned and the investments she made into other areas. In comparison to the money that she kept for her father, she was getting to that level on her own, but still had so far to go.

The money she made was peanuts to the millions Mitch checked in yearly. If anything, all that her father had provided her, was the most important pieces to help her get ahead. And she missed his handouts. She wanted to put everything back in place and continue getting the benefits that Papa Bear had to offer. But Tisha's time was concentrated on making things right with Melvin before any reconciliation could come from the differences she faced with her father. Tisha knew the situation was bad. It was serious between her and her father. Especially so now that she's pregnant. With a baby from dude that her father despises. Not to mention the fact that somebody got killed. Her own flesh and blood. And her father knew who did it, rather she knew it or not that he did.

Her intentions were to get Melvin to hear her out on a few things, even if that meant she had to lie to make it appear like she was taking care of her issues with her father and no longer needed him and his support. She wanted to tell him face to face again, that she made the choice to be with him. This was to be against anything or anyone.

Nothing would come between them again, she wanted to let him know. She thought she was madly in love with Melvin. She was carrying his baby in her womb, a son. And she desperately wanted to make things right, out of the fear of being left all alone to raise three kids by two different men with one who was dead, and the other 1, marked for death. Tisha wouldn't have a problem blatantly lying to the two most important men in her life presently. This was her own father, and the father of her son. If lying would help her finally get ahead in life and situated in a good space mentally, spiritually, and financially, then she was all for it. She would do what she had to do. So be it.

Chapter 20

ONE day, out of frustration and impulse, Tisha up and took a ride over to the house where Melvin's mother lived that now belonged to him. At no time had Tisha ever met, Sherita, Melvin's daughter. She only knew her name, and had seen a picture of her. But indeed, Melvin was still around in Miami, and was out and about with his cousin Vick on this day. Sherita was there. She had long been taught by her father to never give out his number to anyone, and to never contact him directly in the presence of someone who approached and was trying to get her to do so.

Her instructions were to let whoever know that she would eventually get in touch with him, and to let them know that she would pass along the message.

Tisha pulled up to the house. She took notice of Melvin's Tahoe in the driveway. She got out of her Range Rover Sport, the one that still had the tracking device attached to it, and waddled her pregnant self to the front door. She knocked and waited for someone to approach from the inside. The noise from the interior indicated that someone was there. She was hoping that Melvin was there, or at least his mother. It will be a pleasure to meet her again, Tisha thought. She had no knowledge that the old was dead.

Sherita opened the door. "May I help you?" she asked Tisha.

Tisha gave her a puzzled look. She didn't initially recognize Sherita. Tisha had been shown a picture of her by

Melvin, but it was one from when she was younger, more like ten years younger. She was a twelve-year old teenager at the time the photo was taken.

Who the fuck is she? I hope this ain't a new girlfriend Melvin done abandoned me to be with! He's left me pregnant and all! she thought. A rush of rage flushed across her face.

Sherita was able to catch Tisha's demeanor of outrage. It caused her to ask again, "Miss, may I help you?"

Tisha eventually broke her impulsive mindset and defused the aggressive daze. In the process of answering the question asked by Sherita, Tisha finally came around to realize that she was talking to the man's daughter. "Oh, yes, hey! How are you? I'm trying to locate Melvin. This is his mother's house, right? Miss Irene?" Tisha asked.

"Uh, yes, it is. But unfortunately, Melvin, my dad, isn't here at the moment. And his mother, my grandmother, Miss Irene, she just recently passed away," Sherita replied.

"Oh, no! I'm sorry to hear that. My deepest condolences. And would you happen to be Sherita, his daughter?"

"I am, and you are?"

"It's nice to finally be able to meet you in person. Sherita, I'm Tisha."

Sherita simply stood motionless and looked on at the female who showed up at their house looking for her father. With the daughter knowing her dad the way that she did, she felt that there was something off about the picture. At no time had any female ever just pulled up out of the blue as Tisha had, looking for her dad, and he wasn't there, or the visitor hadn't called beforehand to notify that they'd be stopping by. Sherita just continued to keep quiet and look at Tisha, awaiting her to speak more about what potentially it was that she wanted with her dad.

"If you don't mind, could you please let him know that Tisha came by? And it's very important that we talk? And if you will, would you give him this number for me please? I got a second phone now," Tisha said as she extended a piece of paper to Sherita. It had her second line number wrote on it.

"I can do that for you. It's not a problem," Sherita responded and accepted the information.

"Thank you so much. And again, it was nice to meet you. Take care, okay?"

"You as well."

Tisha turned and began to head back to her vehicle. Sherita looked on at her in wonder until Tisha reached her truck, opened the door, got in and started it once more, and drove away.

Next, a mental note was made by her to be sure to question her dad about a few things related to the pregnant woman who came by to check for him. There was a specific reason why this woman would do so. And Sherita, was determined to know the reason why. She wasted no time picking up the phone and texting her dad.

Sherita: Hey! Daddy, please call me ASAP! No, not an emergency in the sense. But one of the weirdest things just happened.

Melvin's phone vibrated on his hip. He took a look at the screen and noticed it was his daughter who was contacting him. What in the world is it Sherita want? he thought to himself. He opened the text and began to read. Once done, he called her to talk about whatever it was that was weird that had not too long ago happened.

"Hey, Dad," she answered with positive, bright energy.

"What's up, baby girl? What's on your mind? Everything good?" Melvin replied.

"Oh, yeah. Everything's good. No emergency or anything like that. But I wanted to ask you something. Is it anything you wanna let me in on about you?" she asked, smiling gleefully as they Face-Time one another.

"Wait, why you ask that? Why you say that like that?" He returned the smile the same from that point. He had a good feeling, judging by the way his daughter was appearing to be humorous, that whatever she wanted to ask him about, had something to do with a woman.

"What up, baby?" His smile was still wide. "I wanna know about this weird thing you brought to my attention."

Sherita continued to look at her father and maintained a strong smile. She then went on to tell him about the visitor that had stopped by looking for him. "Daddy, you got a baby on the way or something?" she asked.

"Huh?!"

"I said... do you have a baby on the way?" Her smile was still wide.

"Why you asked that? I ain't got no baby on the way. And I don't know anything about Traci being pregnant. Did she call you and say something like that?"

"No, Daddy. It wasn't her. It was some other girl. A pregnant girl. She stopped by today looking for you. It wasn't even five minutes ago," Sherita revealed.

"What?!" he let out in shock of the news.

"Yeah, she left her number for you to call and all. And she never said she was pregnant by you. I just assumed that. Why else would a woman, pregnant at that, drop out of the sky to a man's house looking for them? That's too much of a coincidence, ain't it," Sherita remarked. She'd forgotten to mention a name.

Melvin began to brainstorm on the few women he'd had unprotected sex with since his release. There had only been three. So it wouldn't take him long to figure out exactly who it was. But seriously, he thought that maybe Traci and his daughter were playing some type of prank on him. And at the same time, it was Tisha, who he honestly felt that it could have been. He just didn't want to admit this to himself.

"What was the girl's name, Rita?"

"She said her name was Tisha. Some cute dark-skinned girl. She said something about it being an urgent issue, and you need to get in touch with her."

"I figured that's who it was," he mumbled underneath his breath. "Was it anybody else with her?"

"No. Just her. All by her pregnant self. And you do know her, huh?"

"Yeah, I do. But look, text me the number she left with you, okay? And I'll call you back shortly," Melvin lastly said to his daughter. He was now anxious as ever to get off the phone with Sherita and immediately contacted Tisha. He began to think deeply over the newly presented situation he had on hand to grapple with.

Melvin was the main person who knew that Mitch was the one responsible for the murder of his mother. And Mitch was the only one that Melvin was determined to hit. So now, the only thing that Melvin had left to find out was, did Tisha really know how serious the situation had become between her father and him? He hadn't talked to Tisha in months, since the night of the shootout inside the duplex. And he knew that the possibility did exist.

Tisha may not have known anything about who put the intruders up to trying to pull off the home invasion, or, who the guy was that was killed, or what her dad did with the body when she told him about the incident and he went to check things out. The truth was that, Melvin himself didn't know that the guy he killed was related to Mitch until he got the text message to confirm.

The facts was, he was able to put two and two together and concluded that Mitch had to be the one to hire the hitter who took the life of his mother. Who else could it have been? And on top of that, at the time when he returned to Miami to bury his mom, he took notice that the phone book and address journal were both missing. Those were two areas where his mother kept all of his contact information. He knew that the killer had to have gotten his hands on them and later passed it on to Mitch. How else did Mitch get a contact number for him, and he'd changed it so that Tisha wouldn't know it?

Melvin knew that if Tisha had known anything about how serious this shit had gotten between him and her dad, she would stay away completely, out of fear of her own life being in danger. Pregnant or not, this was a dangerous matter to work through. And on the other hand, he'd asked Mr. Raymond to utilize whatever contact he had for law enforcement on the inside to find out if a call was made about a homicide victim being shot at the location in South Miami Heights? Also, to find out if there were any warrants issued for his arrest? There weren't any calls made, and there were no warrants put out. Melvin was good to go.

Damn! What's this all about?! Tisha just up and out of the blue stopped by the house looking for me, Melvin thought to himself. She can't possibly know nothing about how for real the beef is between me and her dad. Not in the least. Because if she do, she just gotta be plain crazy to come by my way trying to talk or anything else. But it ain't but one way to find all this out. She may know. Let me call this bitch right now and see what the fuck she got going on. After all, she might actually be pregnant with my baby like she said she was. Because when she first brought it to my attention, I didn't believe her. I don't know for sure, and if she is, I hope to God that I got a son on the way. I'll name him after me. Melvin smiled at his thoughts that passed through his mind.

He finally opened the text message that his daughter sent him containing Tisha's number. He saw that it wasn't the same one from before. She'd changed it. Or either bought a new phone, he thought. Melvin used the TextNow app to message Tisha.

Melvin: Hey, what's up? It's me, Melvin. I got your message. What's good?

Not even a minute afterwards, Tisha replied.

Tisha: Hey, Melvin, it's nice to finally hear from you again. I never thought for once that you would be the one to abandon me and leave me pregnant to do this all by myself.

But hey, shit happens, right? Can you please call me? We seriously need to talk.

Tisha was so caught up in her feelings and emotions that she never gave it a thought to simply call him once he sent the text message. Her reply was more of a release than anything.

"Fuck it," Melvin said aloud. He then palmed his phone and made the call.

"Hello," Tisha answered. Her voice was a mixture of sultry and bitterness. Nonetheless, It was humble.

"How are you?" Melvin had the compassion to ask.

"I've been making it. Although at times, it got really emotional for me along the way. But look, Melvin, I'm still trying to figure it out, how you, as a man, gonna get me pregnant, then up and leave me the way you did?"

"Tisha, I don't know what to say to help you understand how serious the situation got for me after the shit happened," he spoke in a cautious way. There was the fear that Tisha could have been recording the conversation. She had to earn his trust again.

Melvin also held the thought that she had him on a speakerphone and her dad was there listening to everything. He didn't know what to believe or what to make of her until he knew all over again.

"And you don't think that it was a serious situation for me too? I don't know who that was that tried to rob us or wanted to kill us. I've been in constant fear myself ever since," Tisha retorted. Through her words, she confirmed for him half of what it was that he was trying to find out. And in order to get confirmation on the other half, all he had to do was let her talk more.

"Tisha, check this out. Let's not overlook the fact that I did almost two decades in prison. That's twenty years of my life I spent in a hellhole like environment. It's twenty years of my life that I can't get back. So, it ain't no way I'm going back to that. Especially not so, behind defending myself and standing my ground. Whoever them niggaz was, they kicked in the back door where we lived; and they forced us to shoot it out with them. What other choice did I have?" he stated empathetic.

"I understand, baby. You make a good point, a really good point. And yes, I did tell my daddy to go over there to the apartment just like you told me to. And he did. I don't think he called the police either."

"Nah, he didn't." Melvin chimed in to say. He was already informed by Mr. Raymond through his inside connections that no reports were ever made.

"Well, that's a good thing. And I assume that my daddy and his boys got rid of the dead body and cleaned up the place afterwards. I don't really know. All I did was tell him and left it alone. I ain't even been back that way toward the duplex since that night. And I ain't ask my dad no questions. And I haven't spoken on it no more. I simply forgot about it. My daddy seemed to have done the same. He never brought it up to me again. Maybe this was better to protect me. The less I knew, the better, I guess," Tisha informed in a serious and sincere tone.

Melvin didn't detect any shadiness in her words and came to the conclusion then and there that Tisha wasn't conspiring with her father to do him any harm. Everything was all on Mitch. But the lingering question that Melvin fought with was, who exactly was those dudes Mitch sent? Who was they to him? Who the fuck broke in and came for him? Were they family members of Mitch, or were they simply paid hitters who showed up to do work? This was the last remaining piece of the puzzle. He was eager to find out.

"So, what's the situation between you and your dad?" he asked. "Is he still on that stupid shit, trying to control you and choose who you be with?" he asked.

"I've been making it so far without him. I don't need him now. My hair salon and my other businesses bringing in enough money for me to take care of me and my two kids.

And eventually, the one I got on the way, if you decide not to act right," she stated.

Damn, I almost forgot about Tisha being a boss lady of her own making. She got her own money, Melvin thought.

"And you know I still make a few dollars in other areas too," she said, referring to the streets. "The cousin that I had, who used to take care of things for me in this area, somehow, got himself caught up in a street beef and was shot and killed. My family sent his body back to our homeland in Haiti. But since, I had one of my other cousins to get in rotation with me, he official too. But my other cousin, the brother of the one that was killed, he said that he, my dad and them, ain't gonna stop or take any breaks in between, until the niggaz responsible for killing his brother, is dead, and their family dead. Vino mean that shit too. That nigga ass crazy!" Tisha said.

"Root work?" Melvin asked.

"My family Haitian. We practice voodoo; root work is a part of our culture," Tisha stressed with the emphasis to help Melvin understand clearly. "My grandma is a high-ranking voodoo priestess. Baby girl know her way through and around the spiritual world if I have to say so myself. This how my family stays protected in all that we do."

"I'm somewhat in the know about this type of work. Not too much, but enough. And the way you say it, that makes me believe that you really telling me I better think twice before I ever decide to stop fuckin' with you, huh?"

"That might be part of what I'm saying," she let out with a drop of playfulness in her voice. "But anyways, I finally had the chance to meet Sherita, your baby."

"Yeah, so I was told."

"It wasn't the way that I had imagined meeting the big sister of my unborn son, but I—"

"Oh, you having a boy?!" Melvin excitedly exclaimed, cutting her words short in the process.

"Yes, I am. So, I finally got your full attention, huh, I see." She took notice of how ecstatic he had become.

"Tisha, you always had my attention. I was only scared about a few things. I had good reason to be."

"But how you just up and leave me like that, Melvin? If I have always had your attention, like you say. That's not how no real man responds to a woman who has his attention? I had it hard for a moment. Especially from an emotional standpoint. And not only that. I took sides with you against my fucking daddy, bro! And this how you repay me? This the thanks I get?! You just abandoned a bitch! Pregnant and all, with your baby. That's fucked up, Melvin! It really is, bro," Tisha stated in a serious tone of voice. She began to cry. Her depression kicked in momentarily.

Melvin was made to feel guilty. This was a low point for him. He needed to make it right. His silence continued as he listened on to Tisha relieve her emotions over the phone.

"And I'm sorry to hear about your mother passing away."

He couldn't help but to jar his head at her words. He wanted to say something to this, but he continued to keep silent and waited to see what she might say next.

"Sherita was the one who told me about your mother," Tisha said.

Melvin exhaled lightly, as if he was relieved to know that the possibility didn't exist that he would have to kill Tisha too, at the point when he is to kill her daddy, because without a doubt, she was certainly going to be dealt with, had she let out anything that would have suggested that she knew something about Mitch putting a hitter up to killing his mother.

"So, you say you and your dad still not talking, huh?"

"No. Not really. I haven't even been by his house. And he ain't so much as been by mine. We don't talk," she said. "But Melvin, you gotta understand something. My dad can be a very stubborn man when he wants to be. And I mean stubborn to a fault! This is basically what's going on between us. But I couldn't care less. To hell with him and his backward ways. I gotta do all I can as a woman to repair what you and I have had. This gotta be long before our baby arrives."

"I can agree to that. I'm with you, Tisha," he responded. Anything related to the topic of his son he had on the way was something to humble him.

"Are you? Are you back in Miami. Or are you still somewhere else?"

"I'm still out of town," he said, lying through his teeth.

"Well, when will we be able to see each other so we can talk. And not to mention the fact that I need some dick too! A bitch ain't had none since you left me that night! And I need it in a major way," Tisha said. Both had to laugh at her humor and her wits to ease the tension.

"I'll be back down that way soon, babe. I'mma just show up at your house one night, okay? So, to answer your question, we'll see each other soon. And does Chioma still help you out with the kids like she used to?" Melvin asked.

"Yep, she's been on my side about everything. Daddy pissed her off with him too. So you ain't gotta worry about her running back to tell him anything. If she sees you over here when you decide to just show up one night, you good on that," Tisha replied.

Melvin leaned back against the sofa. He was at Vick's house. He thought over everything he and Tisha had just said to one another. "Look, I'mma call you again tomorrow, sweetie. Okay?"

"Please do. And it was nice to talk to you again, Melvin. It really was."

"Likewise, baby. Talk to you later," he lastly said then ended the call.

Melvin didn't detect anything fishy in Tisha's words. There was nothing out of the ordinary, not one thing to be concerned about. She didn't even give off any signs to suggest that her intentions was to set him up. She basically wanted to be back in his life and couldn't understand at all why he had chosen to abandon her the way that he had. But at the point of him offering an explanation, Tisha was able to reason with him and didn't feel some type of way anymore.

When all was said and done, he was intent on doing exactly what he told her he was going to do, pull up unannounced at her house one night, and they would finally have the long awaited conversation that needed to be had. Maybe after that, they would be able to make a move again on a peaceful level.

Chapter 21

THE day was upon them to meet for dinner, Yolanda and Mr. Raymond. The long hiatus was no more. The government had regrouped and was eager to proceed with the new program. They now had additional work to be done. To derail the ambitious rookie politician before he was to strike at luck and catch lightning in a bottle and actually be elected mayor of Miami. Power was something that the government was aiming to take from him.

Mr. Raymond had highly respected the way that Yolanda conducted and handled business for him. He trusted her probably more than he trusted anyone else that had worked for him, even Emanuel.

At the club's sale, Yolanda was the only somebody that had a stake in the business and wasn't getting over on him in any type of way. Mr. Raymond didn't fuck her over out of the profit money she gained over the few years of being a part of the team. Atop this, Yolanda was a unique challenge for Mr. Raymond, in a personal way.

She excited him because he wasn't able to have his way with her how he saw fit as with the other females he had in his life, and he couldn't control her. She never gave up the thrill of having him continue to chase. His nose was open wide for her. He lusted and desired Yolanda, so much to the point of never turning her down for anything she'd asked him for.

Mr. Raymond had conceived the thought that the more he tied her close to him, the stronger the possibility it would be for him to finally have sex with her.

Throughout the many conversations they'd had in the office at the club, Yolanda had clearly laid out to Mr. Raymond on exactly how things would be and how they would go in the next relationship she was to involve herself in.

Of course, this was part of the role she had to play as a federal mole, but at the same time, this did relate to her actual life. She desired to be a married woman. She wanted her own husband and not need to borrow the hubby of some other woman. These were hints to Mr. Raymond—the married man—that she wouldn't allow herself to be used as a sex toy by him, and to also let Mr. Raymond know in a silent way, that she knew he had a wife, and that the wife, Christine, wasn't going to be let loose from his life anytime soon. Divorce was something Mr. Raymond couldn't afford to go through with his wife. It was too late in the game for this. Yolanda knew that the wife had to have known entirely too much about her husband's activities, both in the legal world and in his illegal realm.

The intentions of the Feds were to nab the wife at some point and flip her to becoming a cooperating witness. They knew that the wife could provide an abundance of damaging information on the suave kingpin turned mayoral candidate.

The bottom line was that, Mr. Raymond was in no type of position of advantage to swap his wife for Yolanda. Besides, any sweet talking or flirting done by Yolanda with Mr. Raymond or toward him, was only smoke being blown by her, to keep her true identity concealed.

Yolanda met with Mr. Raymond and the others at the Bourbon Steakhouse by Michael Mina located in the South Beach area.

The sidepiece, Felicia, and the bodyguard, Willie, were present. Everyone was familiar with one another already.

While enjoying their meals and anticipating the alcoholic drinks that were to follow, a conversation began with Mr. Raymond about the coordinated work he wanted Yolanda and Felicia to perform together on the campaign trail.

"You know, I feel fortunate in a way to have the both of you back together and working once again with each other. K.O.D. really had it going on when the both of you managed the girls that were brought in to work with y'all", stated Mr. Raymond.

Yolanda and Felicia looked at one another and smiled. "Lisa and I are very familiar with how to work with one another and how proper to handle your business, Mr. Ray," Yolanda said. "In fact," she continued on, "I was the one to recruit Lisa. I brought her to you, remember?"

"Oh, yeah, that's right. You were the one who brought Lisa to me to be part of the K.O.D. family. You sure was. And now, like I said, I'm able to have both of you working together yet again. And with that being said, this is how I want us to move forward with things. I switched political parties at the last minute. I'm running as a Democrat now, and I know from the times past that traditionally, Miami has always preferred a Republican leader over the municipal building. But it's not like this will be impossible for me and my campaign to adjust to and overcome," Mr. Raymond said.

Yolanda had a good inclination that the language Mr. Raymond was speaking at the moment came out as complete Yiddish to Felicia. It flew over her head without her knowing a thing that they were saying. Felicia knew nothing past Ebonics, slang, or ghetto talk, and weaves and wigs. The reality of the situation was that, Felicia, in all her glory with Mr. Raymond, was simply all ass and no brains. She was nothing academically, as her level of learning and IQ were below average.

The only thing she was good for in the life she lived was pleasing Mr. Raymond sexually. This was any time he wanted it. Mr. Raymond made the terrible mistake of getting in and going too deep with Felicia and what they had. He'd gotten hooked on her and may have fallen in love even with the sexual prowess and power she held over him. Physical and psychological abilities, was two qualities she'd learned how to use at an early age.

Throughout their relationship, Felicia was able to learn a great deal of the business Mr. Raymond had his hands on, and in the underworld. If she so chose to, she could easily blackmail him and force him to pay any demand she may make. And to prevent himself from one day having to have her killed, because he really liked her, he had her to tag along with him and performing certain duties that was within her mental capabilities.

Mr. Raymond didn't want to create a problem between him and Felicia by bluntly telling her that now Yolanda was back around, her management position on the campaign team, no longer belonged to her. It was Yolanda's. So, with that, he had to only set things to where he could make Felicia feel inferior to Yolanda, and from there, she was subject to willingly giving passes to the credentials Yolanda had over her. Experience and management qualified her more than Felicia.

Mr. Raymond knew exactly what to do and where to start with making Felicia feel small. "So, Lisa, exactly how much experience do you have in holding the position of a manager?" he asked her. She was put on the spot. "My reason for asking is because, at the point of me officially submitting my name and profile to the DNC, they're gonna drill you and me both with tough questions throughout the confirmation process," he said. Whether, this was true or not remains to be seen.

"What's the DNC, that's gonna be drilling us with questions?" Felicia asked with a hint of ignorance.

"The DNC 1, sweetheart, is the Democratic National Convention that we're gonna visit next year during the presidential election. It's controlled by the DNP, which is the Democratic National Party, one of the two major political parties in the country, as I said. I'm a Democrat now, the same political party that Barack Obama represents," Mr. Raymond responded in a politically correct way while looking on at Felicia across the table where she was seated. He was cutting a piece of sirloin steak that he'd ordered as he explained. It was cooked medium rare.

Now was Yolanda's turn to play on the intelligence of Felicia. "Lisa, do you have any knowledge about political science?" she asked. Felicia was seated next to her.

She turned to face Yolanda and began to think over some type of informed answer that she could possibly offer. "Well, my granddaddy was involved in politics as a county commissioner of Broward County. This was when I was young. Of course, he used to teach us all types of things that he felt we needed to know about voting when we was to come of age. But to answer your question specifically, no. I don't have any degrees in that field, nor do I have any experience in politics or on campaign topics. I was under the impression that it may was possible for me to learn on the go," Felicia said to both Mr. Raymond and Yolanda.

Mr. Raymond offered the first response to her. "Yeah, you're right. It is possible you could learn on the go. That's if you were an intern who was fresh out of college with a degree and on the campaign team of someone that needed additional help in some other area rather than in the management department," he remarked.

Felicia simply got quiet and looked on at him in a dumbfounded manner. There was nothing more she could say to combat what he said. Politics were a subject she didn't know the language of. Felicia was forced to stay in her lane.

Mr. Raymond and Yolanda continued on talking. They utilized big words, so to speak, that was above Felicia's head. It was like she wasn't there anymore, as the two cultivated figureheads babbled on endlessly, it seemed, over politics, political history, statistics, analytic, and social issues.

To relieve Felicia from feeling left out, Mr. Raymond finally offered to let her back into the conversation. "So, you see, Lisa," he spoke to her directly, "now the responsibilities required of you being a manager or even a strategist on any campaign team, places a great demand on you. From an intellectual standpoint, you gotta know your stuff, because the ultimate goal is to win. I don't know what losing is. And if I'm lucky enough to make it to the general election, it'll be a one-on-one match between me and the incumbent mayor, a Republican mayor, Mr. Suarez. I'm already aware that it's gonna take a lot to beat that dude. A lot, I tell you. The only real shock that I may have is if death was to overtake him some type of way. Then and only then, might my chances improve," Mr. Raymond stated.

The traits of being cutthroat and treacherous had shown its head in that moment. If not but for words only, Mr. Raymond spoke directly to the things that were in his heart. If he couldn't beat the incumbent mayor one way, he surely could in another way. And that may be to order a top dollar hit on the mayor to rid him of the competitive threat that he posed.

Neither Yolanda or Felicia had any type of way of knowing what type of diabolical designs were formulating in the head of Mr. Raymond. He had the tendency to be a demon about it. There was a set of options at his hands to explore if he needed it. Willie, the longtime bodyguard of Mr. Raymond, remained silent the entire time. He offered no comments or remarks to anything that had been said. Suddenly, he felt forced to say something on the subject. Felicia had a better understanding on how Willie thought on things and how he would jump to a take action to see to it that things moved properly for Mr. Raymond. The trip to Mexico that Felicia was a part of helped her to know what

Willie was somewhat like. Yolanda never knew too much about him in this way.

"Yolanda, you a very smart woman, I see. And based on your career choice to work in nightlife entertainment, people will really be fooled to know exactly how smart you are, compared to what you do for a living," Willie said to her, a rare compliment from a true killer.

This added further insult to injury. The already damage ego and pride of Felicia, was hurt more. And at no time before had Willie ever offered her this type of genuine and sincere compliment as he had Yolanda. Not to mention the smile that was included with it. But Yolanda, was more familiar with Mr. Raymond's other bodyguard, Big Mix, than she was with Willie. Because Big Mix was always on the scene in and around the club when offering personal security, while Willie, was more low key. More of an underworld bodyguard.

Yolanda knew that there had to be more to it than it seemed about the meal that Mr. Raymond had her and Willie come together with him on. There was a reason Mr. Raymond saw to it to bring them together. And she needed to know why. The duty of her investigation made it mandatory that she did so.

Willie continued with what he was saying. "Yolanda," he now spoke directly to her, "I'm more than sure you got college experience, don't you?" he asked.

"I do, as a matter of fact. I actually majored in business and account management. My minor was in public relations. So, to be politically correct, this I'm gonna be doing with Mr. Ray, ties both of them together," she responded.

"Wait. What now?" Felicia chimed in to ask. She appeared to prepare a retort to the words Yolanda so beautifully articulated.

"Being politically correct, Lisa, was what I said. In other words, everything that I was taught while in college, was influenced by politics in some type of way," Yolanda related to the best of her ability in layman's turn to help Felicia better understand it.

"Oh, okay, I'm understanding you now, Felicia expressed.

At that point, the waiter approached their table once more to offer wine and champagne to wash down their meals with. Mr. Raymond, Willie, and Yolanda, all opted to have Cabernet. Felicia decided on a martini. The particular drink offered by the waiter was Chardonnay.

Due to Felicia's lack of proper table etiquette, her ignorance, and being unaware of proper glassware, her dumb ass attempted to have the waiter pour a round of Cabernet into the glass that was specific for martinis. She had no patience to await for her drink she asked for to be served. She wanted alcohol to hit her system then and there. To hell with the restaurants manners and decorum. She didn't give a shit about paying attention to the specific glassware that the others were having their drinks poured in.

The waiter simply paused, put a smile on his face, and awaited the other guests to understand what was happening and correct Felicia from her wayward actions. Mr. Raymond was the one to do so.

"Uh, Lisa? Use this glass here for that type of drink, sweetheart," he said, suggesting with the tap of the glass he was referring to.

"Oh, okay," Felicia responded. She had no choice but to put a smile on her face to play off the ignorance that had been displayed.

Mr. Raymond and Yolanda took a look at one another and smiled. Behind the embarrassment and the humor of it all, they knew that there was additional work that was cut out for them in having to now educate and teach Felicia's dumb ass a thing or two on having class. This was so, to not be put on the spot and embarrassed by her again. Although Felicia had gone to school and graduated, no matter what, class was something she didn't attain at her level. She needed a lot of it.

Chapter 22

MITCH still burn with fury to get his payback against Mr. Raymond over the sucker shit that he pulled on him. He felt he'd been crossed out all around the board. And no matter how it was seen by anyone else who thought of Mitch differently, the only conclusion to it all was that, Mr. Raymond had always thought that he was a weak dude. So eventually, he played him as a weak dude that he deemed him to be.

Mitch was contemplating filing lawsuits and going to battle with Mr. Raymond in the court system. But then, he turned away from thinking this way, once it dawned on him that the club was paid for with the money that came out of the streets. This was drug money to be exact. And also, money that had the life, blood, and the souls of other people on it that they had made themselves rich from. So suing was out the question.

In addition, Mitch knew that the Feds could easily uncover other illegal transactions and other damning evidence through a process of a lawsuit investigation. And he was a die-hard street dude, make no mistake about it. And his thing was that, he wanted to hold court himself in these very streets where he and Mr. Raymond once had a certain level of control over. For a very long time. Also, Mitch knew that had he filed a lawsuit and gone to court for anything, this would be too much like snitching, and Mitch wasn't a mutherfuckin' rat! Not by far. He thought maybe he would have to testify on the stand in front of a jury and would be forced to do all other things that snitches did, had he filed the lawsuit. He also decided against doing anything else that would have appeared to be dry snitching. He didn't want to throw any hints either.

The thing that Mitch did do was, get in touch with his nephew, Haitian Vino, and the both of them came together to have a discussion about it all. What Mitch needed Vino to do was help him come up with different ways he could strike back at Mr. Raymond. Mitch knew that if it was one thing Vino was really good at, it was plotting against the ops. And whatever advice he had to share with him, it would all be put to use.

Vino made the drive to meet with Mitch at his house. Once inside, he took a seat, and they jumped right into the thick of things. L

"So, Uncle Mitch, I really need to know straight from you what exactly happened with the club thing between you and that nigga, Raymond? You never told me the story. You say the reason was, you and that nigga fell out, because he took it upon himself to sell the club, without your permission behind the deal, the part that you had an interest in," Vino stated.

He led out with what he wanted to know. "And the reason I ask that is because, King of Dimez, was doing good numbers. Really good numbers. And at the same time, that was a good way for us to keep the money clean we brought in from the streets. Through the Forex system, to the family that's down in the homeland." The mention of the good days was made.

"You make a valid point, nephew. And I understand your frustrations. But at the same time, you know I had nothing to do with the stupid decisions that that nigga Ray made behind my back. I played no part in the sale of K.O.D. However, this what I do know. The spot we got now, Club Pressure, gonna be live too. It may be smaller and a little less known for now.

But it got the same potential to evolve into something similar to the money machine that K.O.D. Was. And on top of that, Club Pressure, is ours! It belongs to me and the family. It ain't gonna be no outsiders that's gonna have damn thing to do with this one," Mitch said. In a way, he was venting out his anger.

"Indeed, and that's a good thing. But what about the other part that came along with the club business? The connect on the work? The part where we stayed supplied with the product we moving in and the underworld?" Vino asked. He spoke in a way like he was suggesting to his uncle, that although he and Raymond fell out over the club, maybe, just maybe, it wouldn't hurt for him to go back to the negotiation table to work out a deal that would put them back in the loop with the cartel supplier.

"Vino, anything that me and that slime ass nigga Ray had together, is over! That shit is dead to me! And he dead to me. And the moment I'm able to get the drop on that bitch-ass nigga, I'mma put his ass away. Forever! But as far as a new connection to a supply is concerned, I'm working on that. And as a matter of fact, now that you mention it, a few months ago, I had a few of my young niggaz track down one of Ray's men. They took some product from him. And now that I think about it, I might know where that nigga Ray, keeping his supply stashed at. I should have been thought of this shit," Mitch said to Vino.

A spark of excitement was visible on Vino's face. He was always interested in pulling any type of high-level caper, especially against a nigga who was an enemy to the family.

Vino got his start in the robbery business by doing stick ups at the docks along the port of Miami. He never really had to do much in the streets, because the profit money he gained when he and his boys did high stakes capers, was pretty good. The operations that Vino led was on an independent basis, separate from what his uncle had going on as a kingpin.

However, there were a few times in the past when the business of the two would overlap each other. But at no time had Vino gave up the practice of robbery. It was still in him. There was no way he could let himself not take advantage of this opportunity to do a stick up on somebody who had the status as Mr. Raymond, or somebody who put in work for a cat like Mr. Raymond.

With Vino knowing his Uncle Mitch's way of doing things, he knew that there was a definite reason why Mitch brought this to his attention. The specific information that he had been wanted to know about Mr. Raymond, he was now being made known.

"Tell me what exactly you getting at, Uncle Mitch? Do tell."

"What I'm getting at is this, nephew. That silly crane looking ass nigga Ray, running around town, out there lying to people, kissing babies, and trying to live a pipe dream about him becoming the goddamn mayor and shit, ain't nothing but a front. I know without a doubt that he's still tied in some type of way. He simply can't up and get out of the life like that, no matter what. He's still got his hands in on something somewhere. I'm sure of it. And if what I'm thinking is correct, like I need it to be, I know who he's got moving the dope for him now, and I about know who he's got stashing it away for him now," Mitch said to inform Vino.

"Shit, if anything, you should've been brought this to my attention," Vino said.

"Yeah, you right. I should've. But this what you gotta understand. Ray was like a brother to me. And at the time, he was closer to me than any of my actual brothers. Your dad included. So, no matter what we so-called beefing about, we could get past it, because you know I ain't no grimy nigga, Vino. I ain't no snake! And I never will be. And I never wanted to go at his throat like this in no type of way. But now, I feel like I ain't got no choice, not after the fuck shit that that nigga pulled on me, Vino!" Mitch appeared to be deeply offended by what Mr. Raymond had done to him.

"You're a bigger man than me, Uncle Mitch, because had he crossed me out the way that he slime you, I would've been taken that bitch hostage he got for a wife, or, I would've been taken one of his kids hostages and made that clown pay up to get them back. You ever gave that a thought, Uncle Mitch?" Vino said in a sarcastic tone.

He was doing his best to investigate the situation between Mitch and Mr. Raymond. Vino was also putting his uncle to the test to know if or not ice water still pumped through his body, or if Mitch had turned warmhearted to a nigga who literally gave no fucks about him!

"Honestly, I can't say that I haven't, because I have. But the wife and kids, don't got nothing to do with what me and Ray got going on," Mitch said.

"But listen to you, Uncle Mitch. If you was in his position and he was in yours, be honest with me, do you actually think that he'd be saying what you saying right now? Tell me that, Unc." Vino was trying to have his Uncle see Mr. Raymond for exactly who he was and nothing more. Ray-Ray was a nigga who didn't give a flying fuck about him one way or another, his family either.

"You make a good point, Vino. He and I are just two different kinds of dudes. And not only that, I don't see it necessary to get back at him through doing something to the wife or the daughter they got together, Erin. But that son, Ray-Ray Jr., he ain't even worth the mention. That nigga ain't nothing but some ole dick-in-the-booty-ass-punk that so happens to be smart. He got married to an older, rich, white man!" Mitch revealed.

"Say what?! Ray got a son that's a fuck-nigga?! I don't believe this shit," Vino said in shock.

"Yeah, he do. And the nigga was named after him too. Ray Jr. That's Ray-Ray's most closely guarded secret. He don't want people to know he got a faggot for a son. But

Ray-Ray made good use of the nigga over time," Mitch revealed.

"How so?" Vino asked, intrigued.

"He put him through one of the top colleges in the country. The nigga graduated from Dartmouth. That sissy-bitch smart as a motherfucker! He got his master's degree in banking and financial management. He rich. And now that's who Ray-Ray got handling money for him. Ray Jr. and his husband lives out in Napa Valley, California. They own and operate a vineyard and winery that Ray-Ray paid for with money off the streets and from the club. Washed it up for him basically," Mitch said.

"Oh, so they doing it like that. I would've never knew if you hadn't said it. But look, fuck all that, Uncle Mitch! When you plan on turning me loose to handle that nigga for you? That's all I need to know." Vino got right down to business with his words.

Mitch smiled at the eager nephew of his, and his boldness, and level of energy for situation he put on display. The four gold crowns Mitch had on the top row of his teeth shined bright. He began to lay out the plan to attack Ray.

"Like I said, nephew, I know who keeping the work put away for Ray. And I'm also sure that the nephew of his, Lil Phil, is the one getting rid of everything for him and making the money. Lil Phil is the one I'm assuming, that replaced me at the table with the connect."

"Oh, you talkin' 'bout that wanna be flamboyant, arrogant, rich, and entitled-ass nigga that got the triangle on lock? That nigga Twenty-one jump Phil what they call him now. The nigga in the Bentley GT? His dad used to be that dude down on Fifteenth back in the day?" Vino asked to clarify they were in fact speaking on the same person.

"Yep! That be him, Lil Phil, the son of Big Phil, Ray-Ray's older brother," Mitch said.

"Damn! Again. I wouldn't had never known that, Unc," Vino said in slight shock.

"Yeah. That's what it is. But here's the plan. This who the nigga is that I know holding the work for Ray. I need for you and your boys, to go and see about this mutherfucka' right away. He an older nigga. Take him and that wife of his. Beat em' bloody! And do what you gotta do, to force the old man to tell you where the dope stashed at."

Mitch and Vino continued to iron out every detail of the he plot, all the way down to the letter. They couldn't leave any room for error.

Chapter 23

MELVIN was sure to let a few days pass before making the decision to pop up at Tisha's house like he planned to do. His intention was to give the actual impression that he was still out of town. He didn't want her to know the truth, that he had in fact been in Miami for a while, and for her not to put any idea in her head that he had been lying throughout the whole relationship. He didn't want her to find out that he had a relationship with Traci too. One before her.

At no point in their relationship did he ever let her know the truth. Melvin had grown accustomed to doing things on his own time, since being released from prison. For so many years, he was forced to do things how somebody else told him to, and live on a time schedule that the system dictated. Not anymore.

Little did Tisha know, that Melvin made it his business to stalk her and her every move from the day that they last talked on the phone. This took place on a day in and day out basis. There was a need to safeguard himself. He also wanted to be sure that Tisha wasn't trying to cross him out in any type of way, and that she could be trusted.

Again, through personal observation of her movements, he was convinced that she was sincere in her level of affections to do right by him. No signs of being cutthroat or treacherous appeared.

At the time, Melvin was getting around how he wanted in a low budget rental car. He wanted to keep low-key at all costs, since this was how he now had to move, by having a higher position in the ranks with Mr. Raymond.

There was no need to be out in the heavy streets anymore other than touring the city and taking in all the many scenes that there were to see throughout town, with the new protocol he personally put in place on his own. This was to advance himself for his own reasons. It was beginning to prove worthy of something. The less anyone saw him out and about, the more progress he could make in the background.

The time was around ten that night when Melvin drove to the Little Haiti section of town where Tisha lived. He parked the car he drove at a low budget hotel not too far from her house and walked the distance to her neighborhood. He took notice of her Range Rover parked in the carport. The sister, Chioma's Acura, was there too. She was there on a visit like most times, after she got her own place.

Melvin approached the front door, tapped on it in a coded knocking rhythm only he and Tisha knew, and awaited her to come running headfirst to answer like he anticipated her to do. In the beginning stages of their relationship, this was how she was.

The coded ways to communicate were put into place by them. Personal privacy and security for the two, had always been a top priority. And if they were to neglect this, it could spell danger for them, or possibly cost them their lives.

Tisha recognized the knock at the door. "Oh, my God! That's Melvin! That's my sweetheart! I know that knock," she murmured to herself.

She hopped up from the bed, not giving a damn that it wasn't a good look for a woman to be so thirsty over a man, that she'd trip over her own two feet just to get to the door for him. She knew who it was already, and happily opened the door.

"Baby! I knew it was you! I knew you would show up sometime soon," she said with a large smile on her face at the sight of her lover.

Tisha immediately hugged him in a tight coil, once unlocking the burglar bar door. It seemed like forever had passed since she last laid eyes on Melvin.

"Oh, yeah! It's me, sweetie," Melvin responded. The two kissed like they really missed each other, and truly meant it. Melvin wrapped his arms around her growing waistline and her ass, by the guidance of her hands. She loved the way his grip felt on her butt cheeks. The pregnancy had caused her to spread. Tisha got thick. Melvin continued to smile more at the gesture. He thought of how sexually frustrating she had to be.

"Come on in, baby, please. This is your house now too. No need to worry about anybody else," Tisha said to Melvin. She locked both doors behind him and grabbing him by his hand and escorted him to her bedroom. Her emotions and sexual yearnings had been neglected for so long, that the very moment, caused her to temporarily lose control of herself with the obsession she had over him. The tears appeared. It was as if she had experienced some type of crazed sensation over Melvin through her love and infatuation of him. It was truly heartfelt. In addition to this, Tisha experienced a semi orgasm. She creamed herself. Her feminine fragrance filling the air through the thin nightgown she had on. His physical presence was driving her wild.

"Tisha! Baby! Calm down, please. I'm here. I'm not going anywhere no time soon. So be easy," he said to give her assurance.

"Okay, baby. I understand. It's just that I love you, Melvin. And I really missed you so much," Tisha responded.

***

155

CHIOMA THOUGHT MAYBE she'd heard a knock at the door and found her way to Tisha's room to let her know. "Tisha, what in the sugar in my grits, you got going on in here, girl?" Chioma let out playfully with a smile on her face upon peeping her head through the entrance of the bedroom door. She and Melvin made eye contact. He sat along the edge of the bed. "Hey, stranger," she spoke to Melvin. "Long time no see." The two smiled at one another.

Chioma felt a sense of relief about the whole thing herself, because she knew that not only was her sister a happy woman again, but she also knew that Tisha wouldn't continue to be such a moody bitch any longer, because her days of going so long without seeing him, ended that night.

Melvin offered a few words to Chioma. "Yeah, I'm back. And if only you knew how glad I am to be back."

"Well, okay, then. Don't let me hold up the process. I'mma gone back where I was," she laughed and closed the door to give them their privacy. Chioma was eager to get back to watching a TV series she had been watching on Netflix.

Melvin and Tisha got back to giving one another the much-needed attention of each other. He came out of the dark colored tee shirt he was wearing. The tank top he had on exposed the two pistols he had on each side of his waistline. Like before, anytime the two of them were in an intimate moment, Melvin had a tendency to indulge himself in Tisha's love garden how he saw fit. He knew without a doubt, that Tisha was so ready to please him sexually, that she would do anything, especially a blow job.

The sex always came in second place to the head for him. And likewise, he loved to put his mouth on her. He felt the need to go to the bathroom, brush his teeth, take a quick shower, and then, return to her to make love. He didn't want to harm his unborn son. This was 2023, and he was aware of the global contamination in the aftermath of the corona virus, and he didn't want to risk their lives. Melvin was an really clean dude. He rose to his feet to freshen up.

On his return to the bedroom, Melvin found Tisha in nothing but her panties and bra. Her belly was large as she was up in her pregnancy. She was still in the same spot as she was before on the bed, waiting on him. She had time to light up the scented candles and play smooth slow music softly from her phone. There was a Spotify playlist. Her artist of choice was Mary J Blige.

Tisha stood to her feet. She and Melvin hugged and kissed once more. She rubbed him gently all about his chest, arm muscles, and shoulders. "I see you managed to keep in good shape, baby. Do you know how much I missed you? If only you knew. And I love your body."

Her admiration aroused him to sensation. She began to kiss on his neck gently, swiping her tongue in slow, circular motions, making a passion mark on his neck.

"You ready, baby? I wanna suck yo dick for you." Tisha spoke lightly and sensuously in his ear.

"If that's what you wanna do, it's cool with me. Do you, boo," Melvin said, as he stood in front of the queen sized bed with a smile. Just the thought of her wet lips in the head of his cannon made his manhood throb to life. She slowly, with the tip of her tongue, traced the length of his dick from his balls to the tip of the head. He shuddered ecstatically from the euphoric feeling.

Tisha next sat on the edge of the bed and firmly gripped his manhood with both hands, stroking passionately and gently. She could feel the strength of it through the veins as they pulsate and she working him with a hand job. Then, she began to devour his member in her mouth, using a rhythmic motion. She took all of him down her throat. She missed him Melvin so much she didn't know what to do, and definitely wanted him to remember what it was like for them in this way, so to prevent him if she could, from disappearing like that ever again.

Taking long, deep, slow bobs with her head, performing strong suction with her lips and tickling the tip of his dick with her tongue, she was bringing him to the top in record time. The taste of pre-cum mixed with her own saliva, sent her sense of taste into overdrive. The salty yet sweet elixir, deepened her sensitivity in her juicy center between her legs. She vigorously sucked, spit, and slurped, until his thick and creamy nectar flowed to the tip.

She came up off the dick momentarily and spit on the head. She then hungrily gazed into his eyes, locking contact with them, and grimacing in lust, in knowing he was satisfied with the work she was putting in on him. Like an animal with its prey, she played with a dick, going in a lyrical flow of pleasure, from slow to fast, while gripping tight and squeezing. She really wanted to make sure that he knew just how much he was missed. There was no denying this. Not by her actions. The big girl in her wanted to taste every drop he had to offer.

Feeling her own juices seeping down her thighs, she began to massage the sides with her hands in a consistent steady motion, as she gobbled his load down her throat.

"Ahhh... ahh shit! goddamn!" Melvin's sexual moans echoed through the room. "Tisha! Baby! That felt amazing. I fuckin' love you, girl! Shit!"

Melvin exploded all of his thick, creamy, and tasty load into her mouth and on her face. His legs felt like spaghetti noodles once cooked, wobbly and weak. But she wasn't letting go of his dick, as he struggled to gain some sort of composure and try to catch his balance. Tisha was not letting go until he had been drained completely dry.

She looked up at him with a sly smirk. "You enjoyed that?" she said while wiping his nectar from her lips.

"Oh, yes, sweetie! You already know!" Melvin said. But, in the moment also, he had a flashback to the head game of one of his many women, the one in particular named Tina.

Not knowing the thoughts he was partaking in, Tisha said, "That's all that matters. Right now, I'm good myself." She silently hinted at being able to get her own orgasm while she pleased him.

"What?" Melvin said. He was ready to please her body as she'd done his. Her body was extra sensitive now that she was far along in her pregnancy.

"Yes, baby. I done fucked you a million and one times in my mind. Even before you stopped by tonight. I was so ready to feel you, I couldn't wait to cum. Even if it meant by myself," Tisha said.

"Well, I guess that's a good thing, right?"

"A very good thing, baby," Tisha replied. She got up and went into the bathroom to take a shower and left him in her personal domain.

About five minutes later, Tisha returned. They began to have a deep conversation about how they wanted things to be in the future. Now that their baby was on the way, they spoke on many things about their future.

Two very important things had to happen though, no matter what. For one; he needed to be present in their lives once his son was born. And, two, be there with her when she gives birth. Nothing and no one should come between that. By no means. Melvin made this promise to Tisha, and she to him.

Chapter 24

THE old man, Emanuel, was now a target. He had been followed for days by the henchman who was looking to do him harm. The elder was a veteran street legend himself, but became a mortician, falling back from the streets and remaining out the way for many years. He owned a couple of profitable funeral homes that was paid for by the money made by Big Phil in the underworld, his buddy. And now, Emanuel carried on tradition with Mr. Raymond. He was guilty by association. He had no idea that his every move was being trailed by a man that performed kidnappings for ransom. This guy took his work very seriously.

To demonstrate exactly how serious, he was a goon that had placed a tracking device underneath the Cadillac that Emanuel drove daily, a trick that proved to work for him and his team on many occasions in the past. A lot of valuable information was gained by this method put on Emanuel. It was discovered that he would make stops at the graveyard on 135th Street in Opelocka no less than twice a week. These stops would be at odd hours of the day.

Emanuel's place of residence was now made known by use of the tracking device. He and his longtime wife, Emma Mae, owned a home in North Miami, just past Carroll City. They were the only ones that lived there. They had a grown son and a grown daughter. The husband and wife had been together for fifty plus years.

The man behind the order to kidnap the old man and his wife, decided that the best time to have his henchman do the work was at 7:30 in the a.m. This was according to the information Vino had been provided. The old man was most vulnerable particularly on a Mondays at this time. He would leave his house in his car, and head down to the main funeral home in Liberty City.

The plan for the hostage taker was for him to lay low behind a series of bushes that were situated in the front lawn of Emanuel's home. It was a way for him to appear, take him at gunpoint, and force him back inside the home so to take the wife as a hostage as well. The two were to be tied tightly, allowing the proper time for the back up hostage takers to be called on. They would be stationary about two blocks away. From there, the hostages would be moved to a second location, then pressed to give up all the information that the kidnappers wanted to know. If not, they would die.

Like clockwork, Emanuel emerged from the house, determined on heading to his place of business. As he turned to lock the door behind him, the henchman sprang into action. He molly-whopped Emanuel on the back of the head with a mini wooden bat that he had. He then put three more blows on him for good measure.

While Emanuel lay unconscious on the concrete porch, blood gushed forth from the wounds, the assailant opened the door himself, dragged Emanuel back inside by the ankles, then, he zip tied him at the wrists behind his back. A ripped T-shirt was used to gag him and a pair of shoestrings to tie his legs.

The home was a one level rest haven and easy to maneuver through if necessary. The wife of Emanuel got out of bed and was en route to the living room to know what was the reason that he come back inside. "Manny?" she called out, "is that you? You forgot your phone again or something, baby?" she called out to ask. Her feet scurried across the carpeted floor of the hallway. She had on her gown and house slippers. The ski masked hostage taker rushed her at gunpoint halfway to the front of the house. He did it so fast that she did not have any time to even scream before the barrel of the gun was pressed right between her eyes.

The henchman looked her square her eyes. "You know what it is, bitch!" the villain spat and drew back the heavy metal firearm. He came down hard with the bat he had directly on her face, claiming several of the expensive dental implants in the assault.

The old lady was out cold on the floor in the hallway where she too was tied up at her wrists, ankles, and gagged with a strip of an old T-shirt the goon had. He dragged her to the living room and then situated her next to her husband. The hostage taker pulled out a cell phone and made a call to his assistant, who wasn't far away.

Not even three minutes later, the others were pulling up to the driveway to help complete the first part of the mission. Emanuel and Emma Mae were both yanked from the floor, taken a short distance to the car, and then thrown into the trunk. It was now on to the next destination. But before moving out, the home was ransacked. A plethora of valuables were there for the taking. Both the cell phones of the victims were taken as well.

Once the kidnappers had reached the safehouse where they were intended to torture the elderly victims, they were removed from the trunk and taken into the house where the torment was to began. They were slammed hard to the floor.

"Ah!" Emma Mae's arm was fractured behind the rough handling. She yelled out in agony from the pain that she felt. Her cry for mercy was muffled by the dirty, oil-soaked T-shirt she'd been gagged with.

Emanuel, on the other hand, had began to come around again from his state of unconsciousness. He looked around the room from his current position on the floor and noticed that his wife was there beside him and bleeding from a gash wound about her face. Emma Mae didn't have anything to do with anything, but was made to suffer for it all.

The old man had been in and around the streets and the dope game for fifty years or more, operating on a low-key basis and moving wisely. Not one time had he ever been robbed or had he been to jail. Emanuel didn't know how to react and had no knowledge on what to do to prevent the henchmen from possibly killing them both. He would learn all there was to know this day.

The leader of the pack made it his business to smack Emma Mae around more with the pistol. This was a tactic to make Emanuel com to ff any and all secret information he had on Mr. Raymond and where he had the goods stashed.

Emanuel looked on in horror. The assailant knew that in order to get Emanuel to talk like he wanted him to, there was a need to do something as ruthless as he was doing to convince him that it would be best that he did. So, Emma Mae was utilized for this purpose.

A devastating blow with the heavy metal pistol he clutched was dealt to her forehead. The sound was so loud. The left side of her face was split. Blood poured profusely, then the swelling came. The dude then kicked her in the face, knocking her out again. He was a mean motherfucker, and it showed. He showed no mercy to the old lady.

"Hold on, man! Please! Don't hit her no more, alright?! Please!" Emanuel pleaded.

"Say what, old-ass nigga?!" the assailant taunted, viciously kicking Emma Mae yet again.

"I knew I would finally get your attention, nigga!" the leader said in his venom infused voice.

"Come on, now! I ain't nobody but a old man that runs a funeral home and keep busy with my grandbabies when I got the energy to. That's about it. Why y'all doing this to me and my wife?" Emanuel pleaded.

"Old ass nigga, who the fuck you think you fooling? We won't go for just some simple muthafucka! You been in the game for years, cowboy! And we know for a fact you the right-hand man to Ray-Ray Stephens," the masked Haitian Vino said as he searched Emanuel's eyes.

"Man, I ain't got a clue about nothing you talkin' about." Emanuel voice was filled with fear and desperation.

"Oh, you don't? Well, maybe if we go and grab your daughter and those two grandbabies you got, that'll make you change your mind. They can join the fun. What do you say about that?!" Vino spat, ready to torture Emma Mae and Emanuel further.

Chapter 25

VINO walked over, stood menacing at Emma Mae head, and fired a single shot that landed at the left side of her face, causing her ear drum to rupture. Blood trickled down the side of an unconscious and badly beaten Emma Mae's face.

"So, you still ain't got no clue, huh?! And the next shot won't be in the floor." Vino began to laugh viciously. "It's gonna be in her muthafuckin' head! Try me and see!" Vino was serious and ready to do whatever it took to get what he wanted out of Emanuel.

To show Emanuel that he meant business, he fired another round directly at the side of Emma's head again. As she began to come to, she had no way of covering her ear being her arms and hands were zip tied behind her back.

"Goddammit, alright! Goddammit! What you wanna know?!" Emanuel said, desperate to have them stop with the madness they were inflicting, not wanting any more pain and suffering put upon Emma.

"I thought you would see things my muthafuckin' way! Now, what I wanna know is this. Where the fuck you holding all that dope and the other shit you stashing for Ray-Ray?!" Vino demanded.

Emanuel took a long pause and didn't say anything.

"Well, we got all day, old man. This means all day to beat the shit out of you and that bitch of yours there!" Vino angrily spat. He then sat down in a folding chair that was there. His pistol was situated between his legs and palmed tightly, pointed directly at Emma Mae's head. "Oh, so you ain't got shit to say to me on that, huh?! Okay. Fine by me," Vino said as he shrugged his shoulders.

Emma May had blood running down her face. She still managed to look on at Vino, although filled with terror. Her life was seriously at stake.

Vino continued. "I'm more than sure you got somebody at the damn funeral home you own that can bury the both of you pieces of shit. That's if I decide not to have you disappear forever, like that plane that disappeared from Malaysia," said mean, cold hearted Haitian Vino. He stood to his feet again and pinned the barrel of the gun to Emma Mae's temple. Vino was itching to pull the trigger. He had a few words for Emanuel though. "I'm not the kind guy, old man. And I came to learn a long time ago that a smart man, will always know where to draw the line. This should be the point of doing so for you, I would think. This is just a warning."

"Alright. Okay. I'll point you in the right direction. Just be cool. And please don't kill us." Emanuel then complied.

"That's what the fuck I thought!" Vino leaned closer to hear what all the old man had to share with him.

Days before, Mr. Raymond and Little Phil, was supplied with a new batch of narcotics from Señor Chucho. Emanuel, like always, had the duty to stash everything away. There was durable custom made coffins that was to serve the purpose of waterproof corpse holders. Señor Chucho was also sure to provide the Raymond Stephens' organization with a cache of military grade weapons. These were imported from Russia by way of Cuba. There was just over two hundred different firearms and a street value of nearly $27 million in drugs. Only two people knew about the narcotics being hidden in the different grave sites throughout the cemetery, and that was Mr. Raymond and Emanuel, no one else.

"So, where the fuck you hiding the dope, old man? Which ones are the graves where the dope hid at?" Vino felt he was making progress.

"Everything is buried. I got different graves for this scattered throughout the cemetery." Emanuel's tone was one of fear and defeat. He wanted to save his beautiful wife Emma Mae. She didn't deserve any of this. He wanted to save himself too.

"Yeah, I thought you would see things my way sooner or later. You wanna live a little longer and save yo old bitch!" At this point, Vino was toying with them like a cat would a mouse when he caught his prey.

Emanuel was outraged. He recognized just who the vicious assailant was. He also knew who the mastermind was behind this. He'd put two and two together as the assailant knew a lot about his business and the day to day operation. It had to be someone who knew the layout of the land and the whole operation.

"So, tell me, what all kind of equipment will me and my crew need to get the dope out of these graves you talkin' 'bout? 'Cause I'mma tell you right here and right now, you ain't got but one opportunity to satisfy my heart. And if you don't, well, let's just say you won't like the consequences. I promise you... that old bitch, your daughter, and them sweet little grandbabies of yours, all gonna be in unmarked graves. So don't you fuck up!!!" Vino spat. "Yeah, and if you try any bullshit, as God is my witness, it'll be the end of y'all!"

"You gonna need a backhoe and some shovels," Emanuel spoke, sounding defeated even more. He never wanted to betray Raymond and the family. If it had just been him, he would have let them send him to the grave before he would tell them one damn thing. But he couldn't bear to see Emma all bloody and helpless on the floor.

"Okay, I got that part. But what about some chains and nylon straps or some shit like that, to pull the coffins out the ground with?" Vino asked, delighted now that the old man was tell him all he wanted to know.

"Yeah, you gonna need that too. Some thick nylon straps. The ones that come with a crank to them. That'll do it." Emanuel's best efforts to convince Vino was on full display. He had to not only say and do everything possible to save his own life, but also his wife, daughter, and grandkids' lives as well.

Emanuel knew that whoever these goons were that was holding them hostage and torturing them, knew more than they should have about who he was and the operation that only someone on the inside knew about how things worked.

The fact that they mentioned Mr. Raymond by name, let him know that they knew exactly who and what they were talking about. The only thing the old man couldn't bear about the situation was, the hurt and danger that was put on his family. His wife, daughter, and grandkids, had nothing to do with this. His poor wife, Emma Mae, was suffering, all because of the underworld dealings he was involved in.

"Lord, Lord, Lord, please save my wife," Emanuel cried out in agony. He began to think to himself as he watched his wife lay in a pool of her own blood on the floor next to him. Why did I stay in this life? I should have gotten out a long time ago. Why didn't I? Damn fool! Inwardly, he made a plea for God's mercy to shine upon him at that moment, to save the life of his wife. He was ready to accept his judgment day.

"It's a little too late for all that shit, old man! S I'm sorry to tell you, I'm the angel of death. *Malek El Mulk* is my name. I was commissioned by God Almighty himself. Your reckoning is upon you. And now, back to the business. Exactly what graveyard we need to be going to?" Vino demanded.

Emanuel began to relate all the necessary details that were demanded of him. Through it all, he still held on to some sort of hope, that maybe, he and Emma would be okay, and could even walk away.

Vino wrote down every detail Emanuel gave to him. He then spoke to his crew about what all he needed them to do. They communicated in their native Creole Haitian-Creole tongue. Before leaving, they double checked the hostages to make sure they were tied nice and tight.

Vino snapped his finger for one of his men to trade places with him in the chair that was situated in front of the hostages. Stepping out of the room to use his phone, he immediately spoke to the person on the other end of the call. Same native tongue. The call ended. He and others of the crew left the place they were holding their hostages, to go and dig up the graves on the information Emanuel provided them with.

For many years before this day, the stash spots of the graves had proven to be the safest and most secure spots. They kept everything low-key for many years. Emanuel questioned himself as to how exactly had the hostage-takers been able to follow him and watch him like they had?

The poor wife of his continued to lay on the floor, hurt. He continued to pray to God for a way out of this moment.

Epilogue

LATER in the evening, Vino and the others had returned. There was another person that joined them this time. He was the person behind it all. Emanuel recognized him and knew this person very well. Mitch looked down at Emanuel and sneered, then he started to mock Emanuel.

"Well, well, well, if it ain't ole Manny Fleming! I ain't had the chance to see you in person since that day in the restaurant when you and that slimy-ass nigga, Ray, crossed me out and fucked me out of my money and my pride. Y'all really had me lookin' stupid. I hope y'all didn't think I was gonna let y'all get away with that, did you? The way that that went down was foul, because you sided with him. And look what he caused you. That nigga always looked out for himself. Whatever the best interest for Ray-Ray was, is all he cared about. Nobody else. We ain't shit to him but steppingstones. He got you and your wife into this shit, Manny. He left y'all severely open to shit like this to happen. He ain't here to help you now, is he?" Mitch spoke in a smug yet defiant tone. The fact that Mr. Raymond played him like he had, and Emanuel was there to laugh in his face too, pissed him off more.

"Mitch," Emanuel said, surprised that Mitch got the one up on him.

"Yep! That be me, my guy. And if you ain't already figured it out, yeah, I'm the one behind this lovely gathering."

170

"I been warned Ray about you. I knew from the first time I laid eyes on you that you were a snake. If it wasn't for me, he would have been had you killed, you muthafucka' you. I was the one that told him don't do it. Me! I saved your life on many occasions. And you didn't even know you was in danger. And I didn't want or need no police attention," Emanuel admitted to Mitch.

"Oh, is that a fact? Well, Manny, with your dusty old ass, good for you. Thanks, I guess. But, you failed to take heed to one of the forty-eight laws of power, my guy. 'To crush your enemy totally.' Looks like y'all failed miserably at that. Now, I'm back with a vengeance! And want my revenge," Mitch stated.

Emanuel boldly spoke now that he was almost certain he wasn't going to make it out of there alive. "I was glad when Ray took your money and stomped on your pride. Ha, ha. If you only knew. But the best part about this was, when he took your bitch from you, Camille. So, sounds like he took everything from you—your money, your club, your pride, and yo bitch. Yeah, she belongs to Ray now, nigga."

If he hadn't had Mitch's attention at any other time throughout this entire situation, he sure had it now. "You say what, Manny?! Say what?! Run that by me one more time, nigga?! I don't think I heard you correctly. You said, Camille belongs to Ray?!"

Instead of saying another word, Emanuel kept quiet. He still had a small measure of hope left so that he and Emma would make it out of this, and they'd gotten everything they came to get. But he knew street code, and after the venom he just slang at Mitch about Mr. Raymond having Camille as his mistress, this messed up any chance of them getting out alive.

"Oh, okay! Y'all two muthafuckas' had a nice little stash buried in those graves, didn't you. I mean, it was plenty and then some." Mitch smirked at Emanuel.

"Y'all got what you want. Now let me and my wife go. And at least let me get her to a hospital," Emanuel pleaded.

"Ha-ha-ha! You funny as fuck! If only life was that simple, Manny, my boy," Mitch taunted.

"Look, Mitch. You got back all you lost and then some. Ain't no need to continue to hurt me and my wife."

"Manny, now come on. It's simple to understand. We gonna get on your phone that was taken from you, and we about to call that faggot-ass nigga Ray-Ray, and let him know what happened and what still is happening, and let him know we want five million dollars to have you and your precious wife go free from this situation. And if he don't deliver the money, then both of y'all ass gonna be cut up to little pieces. Each and every one of y'all body parts gonna be put into the graves we just dug up. It's simple to see, Manny." Mitch gave his ultimatum.

Emanuel was still laying on the floor, looking up at Mitch. If looks could kill, Mitch would have exploded into tiny pieces. He knew Mitch wasn't going to release them that easily. Because he was determined to repay Mr. Raymond for every foul and dirty deed he'd done to him.

Mitch personally scrolled through Emanuel's phone. He scrolled until he got to the contacts that began with a C. He noticed there was contact information for Camille. He took a picture of all of Camille's information with his phone. He had all the information he needed on her now, to make her pay as well.

"Since she wanna fuck with the ops, I'mma show her ass what it costs," Mitch said as he continued searching through Manny's phone contacts.

He was hoping that there would be a way that he could catch Ray-Ray while he was there with her too. This was personal, not business! And he was determined to make every one of them pay.

He continued to scroll through the contacts, and he discovered others who he knew had to be tied in with Mr.

Raymond in the drug business, Little Phil in particular. A photo of his information was taken as well. The scrolling proceeded. Emanual was simply too old school in his thinking, and in no way, had he gone about handling information correctly. No methods of coding made or nothing. Just straight and narrow.

Mitch spoke to Manny again. "So, Manny, I assume that this is Ray-Ray's number locked in under future Mayor Ray, correct?"

"Come on now. You got sense enough to figure everything else out. Why you can't seem to do that? And the same with this," Emanuel responded sarcastically.

Mitch roared in laughter. "Ha-ha-ha! I love it when I'm in total control of a situation like this one. And I told that muthafucka' before, I was gonna get his muthafuckin' ass! And now, I'mma hit him right where it'll hurt him worst, in the pockets. With his greedy, slimy ass!" Mitch seemed to be celebrating having an upper hand.

Mitch selected the contact then pressed a button to connect the call. Placing it on speakerphone, he leaned down to place the phone in the face of Emanuel. Before an answer was made, he hurried and dropped the call. He then broke the phone by stepping on it several times, and he stopped to pick up the SIM card and place it in his pockets.

"Change of plans. On second thought, let's scratch that idea. I'm not the greedy type like that bastard. Ain't no need for me to chase after more money from that fool. I got more from this nigga today than anyone ever will. And he ain't gonna know who it was that made this move on him until I need him to know. So, fuck him! And you know what, Manny?! I told my boys that one of those graves that we collected the dope from, to leave it open." Mitch was still in revenge mode and wanted to take everything from Ray-Ray, including his dignity and his candidacy for mayor.

Mitch laughed sinister-like, then, he snapped his fingers. Vino pointed his pistol at Emanuel's head. "I left them graves open for a reason, Manny. This was so, for you and your bitch can be buried in them!"

The sound of the gun being fired echoed violently throughout the house. Vino had shot Emanuel in the head. The other goons took baseball bats and beat Emma until she was bloody and unrecognizable.

"Okay, yall, clean this here bullshit up for me. Dump the bodies in the graves that we left open. But before y'all move them, y'all carve them up into pieces. Make sure y'all dump each part in separate graves."

After Mitch guys were to put in work dismembering Emanuel Emma's body, he wanted them to meet up with him once more. "Y'all meet me back at the spot later. Come on. Let's go, Vino." He smiled, delighted in his handiwork. He knew then and there he'd struck at the core of Mr. Raymond's operation.

Mitch and crew had calculated a plan to strike and then later perfected it. Things paid off. The most pleasing part about it all to Mitch was that, Mr. Raymond would never know who it was that got him. He'd never know what had happened to Emanuel or his wife and the millions of dollars' worth of drugs he wouldn't see not a dime from, leaving him to have to go into the money he had supposedly put away to pay back the supplier, Señor Chucho.

The Haitian criminal enterprise that was under the leadership of Mitch was now back in the conversation again in Miami as being the crew to be reckoned with. They were on their way to the top of the underworld food chain. And if anyone, it was Haitian Vino—the nephew, not Mitch, the uncle—who appeared to be the most determined and most ambitious. He was serious about seeing to it that they stayed in their rightful place, at the top tier in the underworld of Miami. Period!

To Be Continued...

Lock Down Publications and Ca$h Presents
Assisted Publishing Packages

Due to an increase in the price of services we have increased our prices. The prices below reflect the price increase as of 11/1/24.

BASIC PACKAGE	UPGRADED PACKAGE
$699	**$1000**
Editing	Typing
Cover Design	Editing
Formatting	Cover Design
	Formatting
	Upload eBooks to Amazon
	Upload Paperback to Amazon
ADVANCE PACKAGE	**LDP SUPREME PACKAGE**
$1,400	**$1,700**
Typing	Typing
Editing (line editing/content)	Editing (line editing/content)
Cover Design	Cover Design
Formatting	Formatting
Copyright Registration	Copyright Registration
Proofreading	Proofreading
Upload eBooks to Amazon	Set up Amazon Account
Upload Paperback to Amazon	Upload eBooks to Amazon
	Upload Paperback to Amazon
	Advertise on LDP's Amazon and Facebook Page

***Other services available upon request.
Additional charges may apply

Lock Down Publications
P.O. Box 944
Stockbridge, GA 30281-9998
Phone: 470 303-9761
Email: lockdownpublications@gmail.com

175

Submission Guideline

Submit the first three chapters of your completed manuscript to ldpsubmissions@gmail.com. In the subject line add **Your Book's Title**. The manuscript must be in a Word Doc file and sent as an attachment. Document should be in Times New Roman, double spaced, and in size 12 font. Also, provide your synopsis and full contact information. If sending multiple submissions, they must each be in a separate email.

Have a story but no way to send it electronically? You can still submit to LDP/Ca$h Presents. Send in the first three chapters, written or typed, of your completed manuscript to:

LDP: Submissions Dept
P.O. Box 944
Stockbridge, GA 30281-9998

DO NOT send original manuscript. Must be a duplicate. Provide your synopsis and a cover letter containing your full contact information.

Thanks for considering LDP and Ca$h Presents.

NEW RELEASES

BLOODLINE OF A SAVAGE 1,2&3
THESE VICIOUS STREETS 1,2&3
RELENTLESS GOON
RELENTLESS GOON 2
BY PRINCE A. TAUHID

THE BUTTERFLY MAFIA 1-3
BY FUMIYA PAYNE

A THUG'S STREET PRINCESS 1,2&3
BY MEESHA

CITY OF SMOKE 1& 2
BY MOLOTTI

STEPPERS 1,2&3
THE REAL BADDIES OF CHI-RAQ
BY KING RIO

THE LANE 1&2
BY KEN-KEN SPENCE

THUG OF SPADES 1,2&3
LOVE IN THE TRENCHES 2
CORNER BOY CHRONICLES
BY COREY ROBINSON

TIL DEATH 3
BY ARYANNA

THE BIRTH OF A GANGSTER 4
BY DELMONT PLAYER

PRODUCT OF THE STREETS 1&2
BY DEMOND "MONEY" ANDERSON

NO TIME FOR ERROR
BY KEESE

MONEY HUNGRY DEMONS 1,2&3
BY TRANAY ADAMS

HUNGRY FOR MONEY 1&2
BY SLIMBOS

A THUGGISH PASSION
KILLAZ ON STANDBY 1&2
LAND OF DA HOOLIGANZ 1,2&3
FRESH OFF DA PORCH
BY IRA B.

COUNTDOWN OF A KILLA 1&2
GUNS DOWN, BOTTOMS UP 1&2
SEX, MURDA AND GOD
BY LO-LIFE

THE LEVEL UP 1&2
BY LUXURY KING

FO'EVA ROLLIN' 1&2
BY ASSA RAYMOND BAKER

HUB CITY MENACE 1&2
BY J. WHITE

KILLA CREW
DYING FOR LIKES
BY ARYANNA

IF YOU CROSS ME ONCE 6
ANGEL 5
By Anthony Fields

IMMA DIE BOUT MINE 5
By Aryanna

A THUGS STREET PRINCESS 3
EMBRACING THE LOVE OF A BOSS
By Meesha

PRODUCT OF THE STREETS 3
By Demond Money Anderson

STANDING ON HER BUSINESS
BY DG SANTANA

GET IT IN SLUGS 1&2
B. STALLS

CORNER BOYS 2
By Corey Robinson

THE MURDER QUEENS 6&7
By Michael Gallon

CITY OF SMOKE 3
By Molotti

CONFESSIONS OF A DOPEBOY
By Nicholas Lock

TENDER
BY KHUFU

THA TAKEOVER
By Keith Chandler

BETRAYAL OF A G 2
By Ray Vinci

CRIME BOSS 4
By Playa Ray

Coming Soon from Lock Down Publications/Ca$h Presents

RAN OFF ON THE PLUG 2 by **PAPER BOI RARI**
STREET REDEMPTION by **TONY DANIELS**
SAVAGE FAMILY EMPIRE by **PRINCE TAUHID**
BAD BITCHES WIT' GUNZ by **DIESEL**
THE SINGLE LADIES by **DIESEL**
COKE BY THE TRUCKLOAD by **DIESEL**
PROBLEM SOLVED by **DIESEL**
TIPPIN' THE SCALES by **DIESEL**
OPPS CRY TOO by **SAYNOMORE**
A GANGSTA'S KARMA by **FLAME**

AVAILABLE NOW

RESTRAINING ORDER 1 & 2
By **CA$H & Coffee**

LOVE KNOWS NO BOUNDARIES 1-3
By **Coffee**

RAISED AS A GOON I, II, III & IV
BRED BY THE SLUMS I, II, III
BLAST FOR ME I & II
ROTTEN TO THE CORE I II III
A BRONX TALE I, II, III
DUFFLE BAG CARTEL I II III IV V VI
HEARTLESS GOON I II III IV V
A SAVAGE DOPEBOY I II
DRUG LORDS I II III
CUTTHROAT MAFIA I II
KING OF THE TRENCHES
By **Ghost**

LAY IT DOWN I & II
LAST OF A DYING BREED I II
BLOOD STAINS OF A SHOTTA I & II III
By **Jamaica**

LOYAL TO THE GAME I II III
LIFE OF SIN I, II III
By **TJ & Jelissa**

IF LOVING HIM IS WRONG…I & II
LOVE ME EVEN WHEN IT HURTS I II III
By **Jelissa**

PUSH IT TO THE LIMIT
By **Bre' Hayes**

BLOODY COMMAS I & II
SKI MASK CARTEL I, II & III
KING OF NEW YORK I II, III IV V
RISE TO POWER I II III
COKE KINGS I II III IV V
BORN HEARTLESS I II III IV
KING OF THE TRAP I II
By **T.J. Edwards**

WHEN THE STREETS CLAP BACK I & II III
THE HEART OF A SAVAGE I II III IV
MONEY MAFIA I II
LOYAL TO THE SOIL I II III
By **Jibril Williams**

A DISTINGUISHED THUG STOLE MY HEART I - III
LOVE SHOULDN'T HURT I II III IV
RENEGADE BOYS 1-4
PAID IN KARMA 1-3
SAVAGE STORMS 1-3
AN UNFORESEEN LOVE 1-3
BABY, I'M WINTERTIME COLD 1-3
A THUG'S STREET PRINCESS 1&2
By **Meesha**

CUM FOR ME 1-8
An LDP Erotica Collaboration

BLOOD OF A BOSS 1-5
SHADOWS OF THE GAME
TRAP BASTARD
By **Askari**

A GANGSTER'S CODE 1-3
A GANGSTER'S SYN 1-3
THE SAVAGE LIFE 1-3
CHAINED TO THE STREETS 1-3
BLOOD ON THE MONEY 1-3
A GANGSTA'S PAIN 1-3
BEAUTIFUL LIES AND UGLY TRUTHS
CHURCH IN THESE STREETS
By **J-Blunt**

THE STREETS BLEED MURDER 1-3
THE HEART OF A GANGSTA 1-3
By **Jerry Jackson**

WHEN A GOOD GIRL GOES BAD
By **Adrienne**

THE COST OF LOYALTY 1-3
By **Kweli**

BRIDE OF A HUSTLA 1-3
THE FETTI GIRLS 1-3
CORRUPTED BY A GANGSTA 1-4
BLINDED BY HIS LOVE
THE PRICE YOU PAY FOR LOVE 1-3
DOPE GIRL MAGIC 1-3
By **Destiny Skai**

A KINGPIN'S AMBITION
A KINGPIN'S AMBITION II
I MURDER FOR THE DOUGH
By **Ambitious**

A DOPEBOY'S PRAYER
By **Eddie "Wolf" Lee**

TRUE SAVAGE 1-7
DOPE BOY MAGIC 1-3
MIDNIGHT CARTEL 1-3
CITY OF KINGZ 1&2
NIGHTMARE ON SILENT AVE
THE PLUG OF LIL MEXICO 1&2
CLASSIC CITY
By **Chris Green**

LOVE & CHASIN' PAPER
By **Qay Crockett**

THE KING CARTEL 1-3
By **Frank Gresham**

THESE NIGGAS AIN'T LOYAL 1-3
By **Nikki Tee**

GANGSTA SHYT 1-3
By **CATO**

THE ULTIMATE BETRAYAL
By **Phoenix**

BOSS'N UP 1-3
By **Royal Nicole**

I LOVE YOU TO DEATH
By **Destiny J**

BROOKLYN HUSTLAZ
By **Boogsy Morina**

GANGSTA CITY
By **Teddy Duke**

TO DIE IN VAIN
SINS OF A HUSTLA
By **ASAD**

I RIDE FOR MY HITTA
I STILL RIDE FOR MY HITTA
By **Misty Holt**

A GANGSTER'S REVENGE 1-4
THE BOSS MAN'S DAUGHTERS 1-5
A SAVAGE LOVE 1&2
BAE BELONGS TO ME 1&2
A HUSTLER'S DECEIT 1-3
WHAT BAD BITCHES DO 1-3
SOUL OF A MONSTER 1-3
KILL ZONE
A DOPE BOY'S QUEEN 1-3
TIL DEATH 1-3
IMMA DIE BOUT MINE 1-5
By **Aryanna**

BROOKLYN ON LOCK 1 & 2
By **Sonovia**

A DRUG KING AND HIS DIAMOND 1-3
A DOPEMAN'S RICHES
HER MAN, MINE'S TOO 1&2
CASH MONEY HO'S
THE WIFEY I USED TO BE 1&2
PRETTY GIRLS DO NASTY THINGS
By **Nicole Goosby**

THE STREETS ARE CALLING
By **Duquie Wilson**

LIPSTICK KILLAH 1-3
CRIME OF PASSION 1-3
FRIEND OR FOE 1-3
By **Mimi**

TRAPHOUSE KING 1-3
KINGPIN KILLAZ 1-3
STREET KINGS 1&2
PAID IN BLOOD 1&2
CARTEL KILLAZ 1-3
DOPE GODS 1&2
By **Hood Rich**

STEADY MOBBN' 1-3
THE STREETS STAINED MY SOUL 1-3
By **Marcellus Allen**

WHO SHOT YA 1-3
SON OF A DOPE FIEND 1-4
HEAVEN GOT A GHETTO 1&2
SKI MASK MONEY 1&2
By **Renta**

GORILLAZ IN THE BAY 1-4
TEARS OF A GANGSTA 1/&2
3X KRAZY 1&2
STRAIGHT BEAST MODE 1&2
By **DE'KARI**

TRIGGADALE 1-3
MURDA WAS THE CASE 1-3
By **Elijah R. Freeman**

MARRIED TO A BOSS 1-3
By **Destiny Skai & Chris Green**

SLAUGHTER GANG 1-3
RUTHLESS HEART 1-3
By **Willie Slaughter**

GOD BLESS THE TRAPPERS 1-3
THESE SCANDALOUS STREETS 1-3
FEAR MY GANGSTA 1-5
THESE STREETS DON'T LOVE NOBODY 1-2
BURY ME A G 1-5
A GANGSTA'S EMPIRE 1-4
THE DOPEMAN'S BODYGAURD 1&2
THE REALEST KILLAZ 1-3
THE LAST OF THE OGS 1-3
By **Tranay Adams**

KINGZ OF THE GAME 1-7
CRIME BOSS 1-4
By **Playa Ray**

FUK SHYT
By **Blakk Diamond**

DON'T F#CK WITH MY HEART 1&2
By **Linnea**

ADDICTED TO THE DRAMA 1-3
IN THE ARM OF HIS BOSS
By **Jamila**

LOYALTY AIN'T PROMISED 1&2
By **Keith Williams**

FOREVER GANGSTA 1&2
GLOCKS ON SATIN SHEETS 1&2
By **Adrian Dulan**

YAYO 1-4
A SHOOTER'S AMBITION 1&2
BRED IN THE GAME
By **S. Allen**

TRAP GOD 1-3
RICH $AVAGE 1-3
MONEY IN THE GRAVE 1-3
CARTEL MONEY
By **Martell Troublesome Bolden**

TOE TAGZ 1-4
LEVELS TO THIS SHYT 1&2
IT'S JUST ME AND YOU
By **Ah'Million**

KINGPIN DREAMS 1-3
RAN OFF ON DA PLUG
By **Paper Boi Rari**

THE STREETS MADE ME 1-3
By **Larry D. Wright**

CONFESSIONS OF A GANGSTA 1-4
CONFESSIONS OF A JACKBOY 1-3
CONFESSIONS OF A HITMAN
By **Nicholas Lock**

I'M NOTHING WITHOUT HIS LOVE
SINS OF A THUG
TO THE THUG I LOVED BEFORE
A GANGSTA SAVED XMAS
IN A HUSTLER I TRUST
By **Monet Dragun**

QUIET MONEY 1-3
THUG LIFE 1-3
EXTENDED CLIP 1&2
A GANGSTA'S PARADISE
By **Trai'Quan**

CAUGHT UP IN THE LIFE 1-3
THE STREETS NEVER LET GO 1-3
By **Robert Baptiste**

NEW TO THE GAME 1-3
MONEY, MURDER & MEMORIES 1-3
By **Malik D. Rice**

THE LIFE OF A HOOD STAR
By **Ca$h & Rashia Wilson**

THE STREETS WILL NEVER CLOSE 1-4
By **K'ajji**

LIFE OF A SAVAGE 1-4
A GANGSTA'S QUR'AN 1-4
MURDA SEASON 1-3
GANGLAND CARTEL 1-3
CHI'RAQ GANGSTAS 1-4
KILLERS ON ELM STREET 1-3
JACK BOYZ N DA BRONX 1-3
A DOPEBOY'S DREAM 1-3
JACK BOYS VS DOPE BOYS 1-3
COKE GIRLZ
COKE BOYS
SOSA GANG 1&2
BRONX SAVAGES
BODYMORE KINGPINS
BLOOD OF A GOON
By **Romell Tukes**

CREAM 2-3
THE STREETS WILL TALK
By **Yolanda Moore**

CONCRETE KILLA 1-3
VICIOUS LOYALTY 1-3
By **Kingpen**

THE ULTIMATE SACRIFICE 1-6
KHADIFI
IF YOU CROSS ME ONCE 1-5
ANGEL 1-4
IN THE BLINK OF AN EYE
By **Anthony Fields**

NIGHTMARES OF A HUSTLA 1-3
BLOOD AND GAMES 1&2
By **King Dream**

HARD AND RUTHLESS 1&2
MOB TOWN 251
THE BILLIONAIRE BENTLEYS 1-3
REAL G'S MOVE IN SILENCE
By **Von Diesel**

MOB TIES 1-7
SOUL OF A HUSTLER, HEART OF A KILLER 1-3
GORILLAZ IN THE TRENCHES
By **SayNoMore**

BODYMORE MURDERLAND 1-3
THE BIRTH OF A GANGSTER 1-4
By **Delmont Player**

FOR THE LOVE OF A BOSS 1&2
By **C. D. Blue**

KILLA KOUNTY 1-5
By **Khufu**

MOBBED UP 1-4
THE BRICK MAN 1-5
THE COCAINE PRINCESS 1-10
STEPPERS 1-3
SUPER GREMLIN 1-4
By **King Rio**

MONEY GAME 1&2
By **Smoove Dolla**

A GANGSTA'S KARMA 1-4
By **FLAME**

KING OF THE TRENCHES 1-3
By **GHOST & TRANAY ADAMS**

QUEEN OF THE ZOO 1&2
By **Black Migo**

GRIMEY WAYS 1-3
BETRAYAL OF A G
By **Ray Vinci**

XMAS WITH AN ATL SHOOTER
By **Ca$h & Destiny Skai**

KING KILLA 1&2
By **Vincent "Vitto" Holloway**

BETRAYAL OF A THUG 1&2
By **Fre$h**

RELENTLESS GOON 3 | PRINCE A. TAUHID

THE MURDER QUEENS 1-6
By **Michael Gallon**

FOR THE LOVE OF BLOOD 1-4
By **Jamel Mitchell**

HOOD CONSIGLIERE 1&2
NO TIME FOR ERROR
By **Keese**

PROTÉGÉ OF A LEGEND 1&2
LOVE IN THE TRENCHES 1&2
By **Corey Robinson**

THE PLUG'S RUTHLESS DAUGHTER 1&2
By **Tony Daniels**

BORN IN THE GRAVE 1-3
CRIME PAYS 1&2
By **Self Made Tay**

MOAN IN MY MOUTH
By **XTASY**

TORN BETWEEN A GANGSTER AND A
GENTLEMAN
By **J-BLUNT & Miss Kim**

HERE TODAY GONE TOMORROW 1&2
By **Fly Rock**

PILLOW PRINCESS
By **S. Hawkins**

SANCTIFIED AND HORNY
by **XTASY**

WOMEN LIE MEN LIE 1-4
FIFTY SHADES OF SNOW 1-3
STACK BEFORE YOU SPLURGE
GIRLS FALL LIKE DOMINOES
NAÏVE TO THE STREETS
By **ROY MILLIGAN**

LOYALTY IS EVERYTHING 1-3
CITY OF SMOKE 1&2
By **Molotti**

THE BUTTERFLY MAFIA 1-4
SALUTE MY SAVAGERY 1&2
By **Fumiya Payne**

THE LANE 1&2
By **Ken-Ken Spence**

THE PUSSY TRAP 1-5
By **Nene Capri**

DIRTY DNA
By **Blaque**

BOOKS BY LDP'S CEO, CA$H

TRUST IN NO MAN
TRUST IN NO MAN 2
TRUST IN NO MAN 3
BONDED BY BLOOD
SHORTY GOT A THUG
THUGS CRY
THUGS CRY 2
THUGS CRY 3
TRUST NO BITCH
TRUST NO BITCH 2
TRUST NO BITCH 3
TIL MY CASKET DROPS
RESTRAINING ORDER
RESTRAINING ORDER 2
IN LOVE WITH A CONVICT
LIFE OF A HOOD STAR
XMAS WITH AN ATL SHOOTER

www.ingramcontent.com/pod-product-compliance
Lightning Source LLC
Chambersburg PA
CBHW071207260626
47162CB00004B/1199